SO-ACH-619

OUT OF THEIR MINDS

and the force of their imagination, men have created countless beings, from demons and monsters of legend to comic-strip characters.

What if their world were real—if dragons, devils and Don Quixote hobnobbed with Dagwood Bumstead and Charlie Brown? Such a world would have its fasinations . . . and its dreadful perils—if it existed.

Horton Smith found out that it did . . . and that he was right in the middle of it!

OTHER BOOKS BY CLIFFORD D. SIMAK

AVAILABLE AS

BERKLEY MEDALLION PAPERBACKS

THE GOBLIN RESERVATION

STRANGERS IN THE UNIVERSE (Selections)

THE WEREWOLF PRINCIPLE

ALL FLESH IS GRASS

OUT OF THEIR MINDS

Clifford D. Simak

A BERKLEY MEDALLION BOOK
PUBLISHED BY
BERKLEY PUBLISHING CORPORATION

Copyright © 1970 by Clifford D. Simak

All rights reserved

Published by arrangement with the author's agent

Originally published by G. P. Putnam's Sons

BERKLEY MEDALLION EDITION, SEPTEMBER, 1970

SBN 425-01879-2

BERKLEY MEDALLION BOOKS are published by
Berkley Publishing Corporation
200 Madison Avenue
New York, N.Y. 10016

BERKLEY MEDALLION BOOKS ® TM 757,375

Printed in the United States of America

1

I kept remembering that old friend of mine and what he'd said to me that last time I had seen him. It had been only two days before he had been killed—on an open highway which, at the time of the accident, had not been as heavily traveled as it was at other times, his car a twisted block of wreckage and the tire marks showing how it all had happened, how his car had struck another which suddenly had swerved out of its lane into his path. Except that there had been no sign of that other car.

I tried to put it out of my mind and think of something else, but as the hours went by and the long ribbon of concrete kept unrolling ahead of me and the springtime countryside went flashing past, I found myself time and time again going back to that last evening I had seen him.

He had sat like a shrunken gnome in the great lounge chair which threatened to engulf him in its pattern of red and yellow tapestry, rolling the brandy glass between his palms and looking up at me.

"I think that we are haunted," he had said, "by all the fantasies, all the make-believe, all the ogres that we have ever dreamed, dating from that day when the caveman squatted in the dark beside his fire and stared out into the blackness of the night which lay beyond the cave. Imagining what might be out there. Knowing, of course, what might be out there, for he would have been the one to know—a hunter, a gatherer, a roamer of the wilderness. He had eyes to see and nose to smell and ears to hear and all these senses, more than likely, were much sharper than those we have today. So he would have known all the things that might be prowling in the darkness. He knew, of course, but he didn't trust himself, he didn't trust those senses. For that busy little brain of his, for all its brutishness, was busily conjuring up other forms and shapes, other kinds of life, other menaces . . ."

"And you think it is the same with us?" I asked.

"Yes, of course," he said, "but in a different way."

A small breath of air had been blowing from the garden through the open doors that led out to the patio and the room was faintly perfumed with the scent of springtime bloom. And through the doors as well came the distant muttering of a plane as it circled over the Potomac to line up for a landing on the field across the river.

"In a different way," he said. "I'd have to think it out. Not the kind of ogres, perhaps, that the caveman dreamed. For his were physical and most of those conjured up today, I would imagine, would be intellectual."

I had the feeling that he was about to say much more about this strange conceit of his, but at that moment his nephew, Philip Freeman, came into the room. Philip, who worked at State, had a strange and amusing story to tell about a visiting VIP and after that our talk had fallen to other things and there was no further mention of our haunting.

Up ahead of me loomed the warning sign for the exit to the Old Military Road and I cut my speed to make the turn and once I was on the road I cut it even further. After several hundred miles of steady driving at a cruising speed of eighty miles an hour, forty seemed like crawling and forty was too fast for the kind of road I found myself upon.

I had, in fact, almost forgotten that there could be a road like this. At one time it had been blacktop, but in many stretches the blacktop had broken up in some springtime thaw and the surface had been patched with crushed rock which, through years of wear, had been pulverized into a fine white dust. The road was narrow and this narrowness was underlined by a heavy growth of brush, almost like a hedge, which had grown in on either side, encroaching on the shoulders so that one moved through a leafy avenue that made the road seem a shallow, twisting ditch.

The throughway had followed the ridgetop, but the Old Military Road immediately began to dip down between the hills and this, of course, was the way that I remembered it, although I had not recalled that the dip had been so sharp once one had left the ridge road, which some years back had been re-engineered and widened into the throughway I had been traveling.

A different kind of world, I thought, and that, of course, had been what I sought. Although I'd not expected to find this different world so abruptly, by the simple process of turning off the throughway. And the world, more than likely, was not so entirely different; it was, I told myself, my imagination that had made it seem so different, a self-willed seeing of what I had been looking forward to.

Would I really find Pilot Knob unchanged? I wondered. It seemed unlikely, on the face of it, that the little village would have changed. It had had no chance to change. It had lain for all these years so far outside the stream of current affairs, so untouched and so ignored, that there would have been no reason for a change. But the question, I admitted to myself, was not so much whether Pilot Knob had changed, but how much I might have changed.

Why, I wondered, should a man so yearn toward his past, knowing even as he yearned that no autumn tree could flame as brightly as it had on a certain morning thirty years before, that the waters of the creek could not run as clear or cold or deep as he remembered them, that much, in fact, of what he did remember were experiences reserved for someone no more than ten years old?

There had been a hundred other places (and more convenient places) I could have chosen—places where there also would have been freedom from the clatter of the phone, where there'd be no memos to be written, no deadlines to be met, no important persons one must know, no need of being continuously well-informed and knowledgeable, no necessity of conforming to a complicated set of sophisticated folk customs. A hundred other places where a man would have time to think and write, where he need not shave except when he wanted to, where sloppy clothes could be worn and no one would notice them, where one could be lazy if one wished, unconcerned if one wished, ignorant if one wished, where a person never needed to be clever and never needed to be witty and could deal in a comfortable sort of gossip that was entirely insignificant.

A hundred other places and yet when I'd made my decision, there'd been no question of exactly where I'd go. Kidding myself, perhaps, but happy in the kidding. Running home, but not admitting to myself that I was running home. Even knowing as I drove those long paved miles that there was no such place as I thought there was and that there never had been, that the years had twisted the memory of it into that pleasant sort of fantasy with which men beguile themselves in thinking back upon their youth.

The day had been moving into evening when I'd turned off the throughway and in places now, when the road plunged down from one small valley to another, heavy dark had started to creep in. Off across the valleys, in the gathering dusk, glowed the soft white spheres of fruit trees in full bloom and at times I caught little gusts of fragrance from blooming trees, hidden from my sight, but much closer by. Even with evening no more than setting in, it seemed to me that I could smell, as well, the strange perfume of fog rising from the meadows that lay along the winding creeks.

I had told myself, for years, that I knew this country I was driving through, that its imprint had so remained upon my mind from childhood that I could drive unerringly to Pilot Knob once I was upon the road. But now I began to suspect that I was wrong. For I had not, so far, recognized one specific feature of the landscape. The general features, surely, for the country was exactly as I had remembered it, but there had not been one specific place I had been able to put a finger on and say exactly where I was. It was exasperating and a bit humiliating and I wondered if this was the way that it would be when I got to Pilot Knob.

The road was bad, far worse than I had expected it to be. Why, I wondered, had the people who were responsible allowed it to get into this condition? The snaking curves that ran along the contours of the hills could be understood, of course, but not the chuck holes and stretches of deep dust, and long ago something should have been done about the narrow stone bridges where there would not have been room for two cars to pass. Not that there were any other cars. I seemed alone upon the road.

The darkness deepened and I turned on the lights. Some time past I had cut my speed, at times creeping along at no more than twenty miles an hour. Those snaking turns were coming up much too fast for safety.

Pilot Knob, I knew, could not be too distant, forty miles at most from where I'd turned off the throughway, and since that time I was fairly certain I had covered much more than half of those forty miles. I would have known if I'd checked my mileage when I'd turned off, but I hadn't.

The road grew worse instead of better, and suddenly it seemed much worse than it had been before. I was driving up a narrow gorge, with the hills crowding close on either side and massive boulders squatting by the roadside, just at the edge of the fan of light thrown by the headlamps. The evening had changed as well. The few stars that had been in the sky were gone and from far off I heard the distant muttering of thunder, rolling down the funnel of the hills.

I wondered if I'd missed a turn somewhere, if in the darkness I had taken a road that led out of the valley. Checking back mentally, I could not remember that there had been any place where the road had split. Since I had turned off on the Old Military Road, there had been this single road, with now and then a farm road coming into it, but always at right angles or very nearly so.

Turning a sharp bend, I glimpsed, off to the right, a low huddle of buildings, with a gleam of light from a single window. I lifted my foot off the accelerator and moved it toward the brake, half-minded to stop and ask my way. But for some reason which I do not pretend to know, I

9

decided not to do it and drove on. If it should be necessary, I could always find another place where I could turn around and come back to ask directions. Or there would be another little farm where I could stop to ask.

There was another place, about a mile beyond —another huddle of buildings crouched against the looming hillside, with a single window, almost exactly, it seemed to me, like the one I'd seen just down the road.

My attention had been diverted from the road for a moment when I first caught the gleam of light from the single window and when I turned back, I saw something coming down the road at me, arrowing down the cone of light straight at me, and for a fraction of the second I suppose I froze at what I saw, my mind refusing to accept what my senses told me. For it was a dinosaur.

I don't know much of dinosaurs and have no great desire to know, there being many other things that are of more interest to me. But one summer, several years before, I had gone out to Montana and spent a week with a team of paleontologists who were happily (and sweatily) digging in what they called a fossil bed, unearthing God know what interesting items and events from sixty million years before. While I had been there they had dug up a nearly perfect skeleton of a Triceratops, and while Triceratops is not so great a find, there being many fossils of them, there had been great excitement because this particular beast had been somewhat different in a vastly technical way from any of the others that had been found.

And here, charging down the road at me, not in fossil bone, but in solid flesh, was Triceratops. He had his head down and the two great horns above his eyes were spearing straight at me and behind the horns was the flaring shield. He was intent upon his coming and had built up a lot of speed and he was so big that he seemed to fill the road. There was enough power and weight behind that charge, I knew, to roll up the car into a mass of metal.

I jerked frantically at the wheel, not really knowing what I was about to do, but knowing, I suppose, that something must be done. Maybe I hoped to send the car skittering up the hillside far enough to miss the charge; perhaps I thought there might be room enough to turn around and flee.

The car spun and skidded, with the cone of light slicing off the road and cutting through the tangled brush and rock of the hillside. I could no longer see the dinosaur and I expected any moment to feel the impact of that great armored head as it smashed into the car.

The rear wheels, in skidding, had settled down into a ditch and the road was so narrow that the front wheels had climbed the bank of the opposite side, so that the car was tilted and I was leaning back in the seat, looking upward through the windshield. The engine died and the headlights dimmed and I was a sitting duck, square across the road, waiting for old Triceratops to hit.

I didn't wait. I slapped the door open and tumbled out and went tearing up the hillside, banging into boulders and bouncing off the brush. Behind me, at any second, I thought I'd hear a crash, but there wasn't any crash.

I was tripped up by a rock and fell into a bush that scratched me up considerably and still there was no sound from down there on the road. And that was strange; Triceratops, moving at a walk, would have hit the car by now.

I pulled myself out of the bush and hunkered on the hillside. The backscatter of the car's lights, reflected off the hillside, lit the road dimly for a hundred feet or so in each direction. The road was empty; there was no dinosaur. But still he must be around somewhere, for there had been one of the creatures on the loose; I was sure of that. I had seen him plain as day and there was no mistaking him. He might have sneaked off in the dark and might be laying for me, although the idea of a lumbering beast like Triceratops sneaking off seemed a bit absurd. He was not built for sneaking.

I crouched there, shaking, and behind me the thunder growled among the hills and on the chill night air I detected the scent of apple blossoms.

It was ridiculous, I told myself, the good old psychological defense leaping to my aid. There hadn't been a dinosaur, there couldn't have been a dinosaur. Not here in these boyhood hills of mine, not more than twenty miles from my boyhood home of Pilot Knob. I had just imagined it. I had seen something else and thought it was a dinosaur.

But good old psychological aid or not, I knew damn well exactly what I'd seen, for I still could see it in my mind, the great flare of the frill, with the coal-red eyes glowing in the headlights. I didn't know what was going on and there was no way to explain it (for a Triceratops on this country road, sixty million years at least after the last Triceratops had died, was impossible), but I still could not accept the belief that it had not been there.

I got shakily to my feet and went carefully down to the car, gingerly picking my way through the loose and shattered hillside stone, which had a tendency to slide beneath my feet. The thunder was louder now and the hills to the west, which lay down the slot of valley up which the road came winding, were outlined every few seconds by lightning flashes. The storm was moving fast and getting close.

The car was jammed across the road with the rear wheels in the ditch and the back part of the body only an inch or two above the roadbed. I got into it, switched off the lights, and started the motor. But when I tried to move it, there was no forward motion. The rear wheels spun with a whining sound, hurling a shower of dirt and pebbles into the fender wells. I tried to back up to gain some room, but the wheels still spun. It became apparent the car was tightly stuck.

I shut off the motor and got out, standing a moment, listening to the pauses between the rolls of thunder, for any sound that might denote some great beast lurking in the dark. There was nothing to be heard.

I started walking up the road, not too brave about it—downright scared, in fact—ready to break and run at the slightest movement in the dark, or the smallest sound.

Up ahead of me I saw the house I had spotted. The

light still shone out of the single window, but the rest of the house was dark. A lightning flash lit the land with a bright blue glow and I could see that the house was small and tumbledown, crouched close against the land, with a crazy chimney that leaned against the wind. Up the hill beyond the house a ramshackle barn staggered drunkenly against a haystack that stood at one corner of it and beyond the barn was a peeled-pole corral that shone like a curious arrangement of bare and polished bones in the lightning flash. A large woodpile loomed at the back of the house and alongside it was an ancient car with its rear end held up by a plank placed across a couple of sawhorses.

In that single lightning flash, I recognized the place. Not this specific place, of course, but the kind of place it was. For when I had been a boy in Pilot Knob, there had been places such as this—hardscrabble acreages (one would hesitate to call them farms) where hopeless families broke their hearts, year after endless year, to keep food upon the tables and clothes upon their bodies. Such places had been in this country twenty years ago and they still were here and times had not really changed. No matter what might happen in the world outside, the people here, I realized, still lived much as they had always lived.

With the way lighted by the lightning flashes, I followed the path up toward the lighted window and finally stood before a door. I mounted the rickety stairs up to the stoop and knocked.

I didn't have to wait. The door came open almost instantly. It was as if the people inside had been waiting for me, had, indeed, been expecting me.

The man who opened the door was small and grizzly. He wore a hat and pipe. The teeth that clenched the pipe were yellow; the eyes that looked out from under the drooping brim of the big black hat were a washed out blue.

"Well, come on in," he yelled at me. "Don't stay gawking there. The storm is about to break and it will wet your hide."

I stepped in and he closed the door behind me. I was in a kitchen. A large woman, with her body proportionately larger than her head, dressed in a shapeless Mother Hubbard sort of garment and with a piece of cloth tied about her head, stood in front of the wood-burning stove on top of which supper was in the process of being cooked. A rickety table covered by a piece of green oilcloth was set for the meal and the light in the room came from a kerosene lantern set in the center of the table.

"I'm sorry to trouble you," I said, "but I'm stuck just down the road. And I would guess that I am lost as well."

"These here be tangly roads," said the man, "for one who ain't used to them. They wind about a lot and some of them end up going nowhere. Where might you be headed, stranger?"

"Pilot Knob," I said.

He nodded sagely. "You took the wrong turning just down the road a piece."

"I was wondering," I said, "if you could hitch up a horse and pull me back onto the road. The car skidded and the back wheels went into the ditch. I'll be more than willing to pay you for your trouble."

"Here, stranger, sit," he said, pulling a chair out from the table. "We're just about to eat and there's enough for three and we'd be proud to have you join us."

"But the car," I reminded him. "I'm in something of a hurry."

He shook his head. "Can't be done. Not tonight, at least. The horses aren't in the barn. They're out in the pasture somewhere, probably up atop the hill. Couldn't pay me enough, no one could, to go out hunting them with it about to rain and the rattlesnakes."

"But rattlesnakes," I said, somewhat foolishly and to no great point, "aren't out at night."

"Let me tell you, son," he said, "no one ever rightly knows about a rattlesnake."

"I forgot myself," I said. "My name is Horton Smith." I was getting tired of his calling me "son" and "stranger."

14

The woman turned from the stove, a big fork held in her hand.

"Smith," she said, excited. "Why, that is our name, too! Could it be that you are kin?"

"No, Maw," said the man. "There is a passel of Smiths. Just because a man's named Smith don't signify that he'd be related to us. But," he said, "it seems to me that this fortunate similarity of names might call for a snort."

He reached down under the table and brought up a gallon jug. From a shelf behind him he picked up a couple of glasses.

"You look to me like a city feller," he said, "but I hear that some of them are fairly good at drinking. Now this stuff ain't what you'd rightly call first class likker, but it is top grade corn squeezings and it is guaranteed not to poison you. Don't take too big a slug to start with or it might strangle you. But along about the third gulp that you take you don't need to worry none, because by that time you will be acclimated to it. I tell you there ain't nothing cozier on a night like this than to cuddle up alongside a jug of moonshine. I got it off Old Joe Hopkins. He makes it on an island in the river . . ."

He had hoisted the jug to pour, but now a startled look ran across his face and he looked sharply at me. "Say, you ain't a revenooer, are you?"

"No," I said, "I'm not a revenuer."

He resumed the pouring operation. "You never can be sure," he said. "They come pussyfooting around and there ain't no way to know them. Used to be a man could spot them a country mile, but now they're getting tricky. They fix themselves up to look like almost anybody."

He shoved one of the glasses across the table at me.

"Mr. Smith," he said, "I am downright sorry about not being able to oblige you. Not right away, at least. Not tonight, not with this storm coming up. Come morning, I'll be purely tickled to hitch up a horse and drag your car out of there."

"But the car is across the road. It is blocking traffic."

"Mister," said the woman standing at the stove, "that

needn't bother you. That road don't go nowhere. Just up the hill a piece to an old abandoned house and then it peters out."

"They do say," said the man, "that the house is haunted."

"Perhaps you have a phone. I could call . . ."

"We ain't got a phone," the woman said.

"What a man wants with a phone," said the man, "is more than I can cipher. Jingling all the time. People calling up just to jaw at you. Never gives a person a purely peaceful moment."

"Phones cost money," said the woman.

"I suppose I could walk down the road," I said. "There was a farm down there. They might be able . . ."

The man wagged his head. "Go ahead and grab that glass," he said, "and put a snort inside you. Worth your life to go walking down that road. I ain't one to say much against a neighbor, but no one should be allowed to keep a pack of vicious dogs. They guard the place, of course, and they keep the varmints off, but a man's life ain't worth a hoot should he stumble on them in the dark."

I picked up the glass and sampled the liquor and it was pretty bad. But it did light a little fire down inside of me.

"You don't want to go nowhere," said the woman. "It is about to rain."

I took another drink and it didn't taste half bad. It tasted better than the first one had and it stoked up the fire.

"You'd best sit down, Mr. Smith," the woman said. "I'm about to take up the victuals. Paw, you hand him down a plate and cup . . ."

"But I . . ."

"Shucks," said the man, "you won't refuse to eat with us, now will you? The old woman has cooked up a mess of hog jowls with some greens and they'll be licking good. There ain't no one in the world can cook up better hog jowls. I been sitting here fair drooling for them to be done." He looked at me speculatively. "I'll bet you never yet have sunk a tooth into real hog jowls. They ain't city food."

"You'd be wrong," I told him. "I have eaten them, many years ago." To tell the truth, I was hungry and hog jowls sounded fine.

"Go ahead," he said, "and finish up the glass. It will curl your toes."

I finished up the drink and he reached up on the shelf and took down a cup and plate and got a knife and fork and spoon out of a drawer in the table and set a place for me. The woman brought the food and put it on the table.

"Now, mister," she said, "you just draw up a chair to the place that's set for you. And, Paw, you take that pipe out of your mouth." She said to me, "It's bad enough he wears that hat all the time—he even sleeps in it—but I will not stand him sitting at the table and trying to fork his victuals in around that pipe."

She settled down into her chair. "You just pitch in and help yourself," she told me. "It ain't no fancy eating, but it's clean and there is plenty of it and I hope you like it."

It was very tasty and satisfactorily filling and there did seem plenty of it; almost as if, I thought, they had expected, all along, that an extra person would drop in for supper.

Halfway through the meal the rain started coming down, solid sheets of rain that hammered at the shaky house, making such an uproar that we had to raise our voices to be heard above it.

"There ain't nothing," said the man, once he had begun to slow his shoveling in of food, "that is better than hog jowls, barring mayhaps a possum. Now, you take a possum and you fixed him up with sweet pertaters and there ain't a thing that goes down as smooth. Used to have a lot of possum, but we ain't had one of them for a coon's age now. To collect a possum a man must have a dog and after old Preacher up and died, I didn't have the heart to get another dog. I purely loved that pup and I couldn't bring myself to get another dog to take his place."

The woman wiped a tear away. "He was the finest dog we ever had," she said. "Just like family. He slept underneath the stove and it got so hot at times that his fur would sort of sizzle, but he never seemed to mind. I guess

17

he liked it hot. Maybe you think Preacher is a funny name to call a dog, but he looked just like a preacher. Acted like one, too, solemn, and sort of dignified and sad . . .'"

"Except when he was hunting possum," Paw said. "He was a ring-tailed terror when he was after possum."

"We never did mean to be irreligious," said the woman. "You just couldn't call him by any other name even if you tried. He looked just like a preacher."

We finished eating and Paw put the pipe back into his mouth and reached for the jug.

"Thanks," I said, "but no more for me. I must be getting on. If you'd let me take a few sticks from the woodpile, I might be able to wedge them underneath the wheels . . ."

"I wouldn't think on it," said Paw. "Not in this storm, I wouldn't. It'd be a scandal to the jaybirds to let you go out in it. You stay here snug and dry and we'll do some drinking and you can start tomorrow. We ain't got a second bed, but we have a couch you can stretch out on. It's real comfortable and you won't have no trouble sleeping. The horses will come down early in the morning and we can catch them up and drag you out of there."

"I couldn't think of it," I said. "I've imposed on you enough."

"It's a plumb pleasure to have you," he said. "A new face to talk with ain't something that comes along too often. Me and Maw, we just sit and look at one another. We ain't got a thing to say. We've jawed at one another so long we have said it all."

He filled my glass and shoved it across the table. "Wrap yourself around that," he told me, "and be thankful you got shelter on a night like this and I don't want to hear no more about leaving here until morning comes."

I picked up the glass and had a good long drink and I must admit that the idea of not going out into the storm had some attraction for me.

"There is some advantage, after all," said Paw, "to not having a dog to go out after possum, although I must admit I sorrily miss old Preacher. But not having any dog

18

gives you a lot more sitting time and I don't suppose a young sprout like you appreciates it, but sitting time is the most valuable there is. You do a lot of thinking and you do a lot of dreaming and you're a better man for it. Most of the skonks you run across get that way because they don't take no sitting time. They're everlastingly on the push and they are running all the time and they think they're running after something, but mostly they are running from themselves."

"I think you're right," I said, thinking of myself. "I think you're entirely right."

I had another drink and it felt so good I had another one.

"Here, young fellow," said Paw, "hold out that glass of yours. You're running kind of low."

I held out the glass and the jug gurgled and the glass was full again.

"Here we sit," said Paw, "as snug as bugs and ain't a tarnation thing to do except to sit here and do some friendly drinking and a little talking and pay time no heed. Time," he said, "is a man's best friend if he makes good use of it and a man's worst enemy if he lets it run him. Most people who live by the clock are miserable sorts of critters. But living by the sun, that is something different."

There was something wrong, I knew. I could feel the edge of wrongness. Something about these two, as if I should have known them, as if I'd met them somewhere many years ago and suddenly would know them and remember who they were and where I'd met them and what kind of folks they were. But reach for the memory of them as best I could, it all eluded me.

The man was talking again and I realized I was only hearing part of what he said. I knew he was talking about coon hunting and the best bait to use for catfish and a lot of other very friendly things, but I had missed, I knew, a great amount of detail.

I finished off the glass and held it out again without any invitation from him and he filled it up again and it all was comfortable and fine—the wood fire murmuring in the stove and the clock upon the mantle shelf beside the pantry door ticking loudly and companionably in the close confines of the room. In the morning life would take up again and I'd drive to Pilot Knob, taking the fork I'd missed. But this, I told myself, was a piece of sitting time, a piece of resting time, a time to sit and let the clock tick on and not think of anything, or not much of anything. I was building up quite a glow from the moonshine I was drinking and I knew I was, but I didn't seem to mind. I went right on drinking and listening and not thinking of tomorrow.

"By the way," I asked, "how are the dinosaurs this year?"

"Why, there are a few of them about," he said, unconcernedly, "but it seems to me they're a mite smaller than they used to be."

And then he went on telling about a bee tree he had cut and about the year when the rabbits, eating loco weed, got so pugnacious packs of them were hazing grizzly bear all about the landscape. But that must have happened somewhere else, for here in this country, I knew, there were no loco weeds and no grizzlies, either.

And, finally, I remember going off to bed on the couch in the living room while Paw stood by with the lantern in his hand. I took off my jacket and hung it on a chair back and then took off my shoes and put them on the floor, squared and neatly placed. Then, loosening my tie, I lay down upon the couch and, as he'd said, it was comfortable.

"You'll get a good night's sleep," said Paw. "Barney always slept here when he came to visit us. Barney in here and Sparky out there in the kitchen."

And suddenly, as those names soaked into my mind, I had it! I struggled to arise and I did get part way up. "I know who you are now," I shouted at him. "You are Snuffy Smith, the one that was with Barney Google and Sparkplug and Sunshine and all the rest of them in the comic strip."

I tried to say more, but I couldn't and it didn't seem too important really, nor too remarkable.

I collapsed back on the couch and lay there and Snuffy went away, taking the lantern with him and on the roof above me I heard the pattering of rain.

I went to sleep with the patter of the rain.

And woke up with rattlesnakes. . . .

2

Fear saved me—a brutal, numbing fear that froze me for that few seconds which allowed my brain to take in the situation and assess it and decide on a course of action.

The deadly, ugly head reared above my chest, pointing down into my face and in a fraction of a second, in so short a time that only a high-speed camera could have caught the action, it could have struck, with the curved and vicious fangs erected for the strike.

If I had moved, it would have struck.

But I did not move because I could not move, because the fear, instead of triggering my body into instant reflex action, stiffened me and froze me, the muscles knotted, the tendons rigid, and gooseflesh popping on my skin.

The head that hung above me seemed chiseled out of bone, sparse and cruel, the little eyes shining with the dull luster of a newly-broken, but unpolished stone, and between the eyes and nostrils the pits that served as radiation-sensing organs. The forked tongue flicked in and out, with a motion not unlike the play of lightning in the sky, testing and sensing, supplying the tiny brain that lay inside the skull with the facts of this creature upon which the snake had found itself. The body was a dull yellow, marked by darker stripes that ran around the body, flaring out into lopsided diamond patterns. And it was big—perhaps not so big as it seemed in that fear-laden moment, while I stared up into its eyes—but big enough so that I could feel the weight of its body on my chest.

Crotalus horridus horridus—a timber rattlesnake!

It knew that I was there. Its eyesight, poor as it might

23

be, still would provide some information. Its forked tongue gave it more. And those radiation pits would be measuring my body temperature. It was dimly puzzled, more than likely—as much as a reptile could be puzzled. Undecided and unsure. Friend or foe? Too big for food and yet perhaps a threat. And at the first sign of threat, I knew, those deadly fangs would strike.

My body was stiff and rigid, frozen into immobility by fear, but in another moment, I realized, even through the haze of fear, that immobility would pass and I would try to get away, try in desperation to get beyond the creature's reach. But my brain, still befogged by fear, but working with the cold logic of desperation, said I must make no move, that I must remain the frozen chunk of flesh I was. It was my one chance to survive. A single motion would be interpreted as a threat and the snake would defend itself.

I let my eyelids slide down, as slowly as I could, so that I needn't even blink, and lay in darkness while bile-tinged gorge rose in my throat and my stomach churned in panic.

I must not move, I told myself. No stirring, not a single finger twitched, not a tremor in the body.

The hardest part of it was to keep my eyes closed, but I knew I must. Even so much as the sudden flicking of an eyelid might cause the snake to strike.

My body screamed at me—every muscle fiber, every nerve, all my prickling skin screamed to get away. But I held the body still—I, the mind, the brain, the thinking. And the thought crept in unbidden that this was the first time in my life that the brain and body had been so utterly at odds.

My skin seemed to crawl beneath the mincing impact of a million unclean feet. My digestive tract revolted, knotting and twisting. My heart was beating so hard that the pressure of the blood running in my veins made me feel choked and bloated.

And still the weight hung there upon my chest.

I tried to calculate the attitude of the snake by the pattern of its weight upon my chest. Had it changed position? Had something triggered that snakish brain into aggressive action, was it even now pulling its body up and back into the S-curve that was preliminary to a strike? Or was it lowering its raised head, preparatory to moving on, satisfied that I was no threat?

If only I could open my eyes and know! It seemed more than flesh could bear not to see the danger (if there should be danger) and, recognizing it, brace one's self against it.

But I kept my eyes closed—not tight shut, not squeezed tight, but closed as naturally as I could, for there was no way to know whether the movement of the facial muscles involved in the squeezing of the eyes tight shut might be enough to alarm the snake.

I found myself trying to breathe as shallowly as I could, for breathing was movement—although I told myself that by now the snake must have become accustomed to the rhythm of my breathing.

The snake moved.

My body tensed at the feel of it moving and once tensed, I held it tensed. It moved down my chest and across my belly and it seemed to take a long time for the extended body of it to travel the entire way and finally to be gone.

Now! my body yelled—now is the time to get away. But I held the body quiet and slowly opened my eyes, so slowly that sight came back gradually, a little at a time, first blurred sight through the eyelashes, then through narrow slits, and finally open eyes.

When they had been open before, I had seen nothing but the ugly, flattened, skull-shaped head pointing down into my face. But now I saw the rock roof that loomed four feet or so above my head, slanting downward toward my left. And I smelled the dank odor of a cave.

I lay, not upon the couch where I had gone to sleep to the sound of rain upon the roof, but on another slab of rock, the floor of the cave. I slanted my eyes to the left and saw that the cave was not deep, that it was, in fact, little more than a horizontal crevice weathered out of an exposed outcropping of limestone.

A snake den! I thought. Not one snake, perhaps, but probably any number of them. Which meant that I must

25

remain as quiet as possible, at least until I could be sure there were no further snakes.

Morning light was slanting into the front of the crevice, touching and warming the right side of my body. I rolled my eyes in that direction and found that I was looking down a narrow notch that climbed up from the main valley. And there, down in the notch was the road that I had driven and there was my car as well, slanted across the road. But of the house that had been there the night before there was now no sign. Nor of the barn, nor the corral or woodpile. There was nothing at all. Between the road and where I lay stretched a hillside pasture spotted with clumps of heavy brush, tangles of blackberry thickets, and scattered groups of trees.

I might have thought it was a different place entirely had it not been for my car down there on the road. The car's being there meant this was the place, all right, and that whatever had happened to change it must have happened to the house. And that was crazier than hell, for things like that simply do not happen. Houses and haystacks, corrals and woodpiles, and cars with their rear ends jacked up do not disappear.

Back in the rear of the cave I heard a slithering sound and a dry rustling and something went very swift and hard across my ankles and lit with a crunching noise in a pile of winter-dried leaves just outside the cave.

My body rebelled. It had been held in fear too long. It acted by an instinct which my mind was powerless to counteract and even as the reasoning part of me protested violently, I had already jackknifed out of the cave and was on my feet, crouching, on the hillside. In front of me and slightly to my right a snake was streaking down the hillside, going very fast. It reached a blackberry thicket and whipped into it and the sound of its movement stopped.

All movement stopped and all sound and I stood there on the hillside, tensed against the movement and listening for the sound.

Swiftly I scanned the ground all around me, then went over it more slowly and carefully. One of the first things that I saw was my jacket, bunched upon the ground, as if I had dropped it there most carefully—as if, I thought with something of a shock, I had meant to hang it on the chair back, but there had been no chair. Up the hillside just a pace or two were my shoes, set neatly side by side, their toes pointing down the hill. And when I saw the shoes I realized, for the first time, that I was in my stocking feet.

There was no sign of snakes, although there was something stirring around in the back of the cave, where it was too dark for me to see. A bluebird winged down and settled on an old dry mullen stalk and looked at me with beady eyes and from somewhere, far off across the valley, came the tinkling of a cowbell.

I reached out with a cautious toe and prodded at the jacket. There seemed to be nothing under it or inside of it, so I reached down and picked it up and shook it. Then I picked up the shoes and without stopping to put them on beat a retreat down the hillside, but very cautiously, holding in check an overpowering urge to run and get it over with, to get off the hillside and down to the car as quickly as I could. I went slowly, watching closely for snakes every foot of the way. The hillside, I knew, must be crawling with them—there had been the one upon my chest and the one that went across my ankles and the one still messing around in the back of the cave, plus God knew how many others.

But I didn't see a one. I stepped on a thistle with my right foot and had to go on tiptoe with that foot the rest of the way so I wouldn't drive the spines that were sticking in the sock into my flesh, but there weren't any snakes —none visible, at least.

Maybe, I thought, they were as afraid of me as I was of them. But I told myself they couldn't be. I found that I was shaking and that my teeth were chattering and at the bottom of the hill, just above the road, I sat down weakly on a patch of grass, well away from any thicket or boulder where a snake might lurk and picked the thistle spines out of my sock. I tried to put on my shoes, but my hands were shaking so I couldn't and it was then I realized how frightened I had been and the knowledge of the true depth of my fright only made me more so.

My stomach rose up and hit me in the face and I rolled over on one side and vomited and kept on retching for a long time after there was nothing further to bring up.

The vomiting seemed to help, however, and I finally got my chin wiped off and managed to get my shoes on and get them tied, then staggered down to the car and leaned against its side, almost hugging it I was so glad to be there.

And standing there, hugging that ugly hunk of metal, I saw that the car was not really stuck. The ditch was far shallower than I had thought it was.

I got into the car and slid behind the wheel. The key was in my pocket and I switched on the motor. The car walked out of there with no trouble and I headed down the road, back the way I'd come the night before.

It was early morning; the sun could not have been more than an hour or so into the sky. Spiderwebs in the roadside grass still glittered with the dew and meadowlarks went soaring up into the sky, trailing behind them the trilling tatters of their songs.

I turned a bend and there the vanished house stood beside the road, just ahead of me, with its crazily canted chimney and the woodpile at the back, with the car beside the woodpile, and the barn that leaned against the haystack. All of it as I'd seen it the night before, in the flare of lightning flashes.

It was quite a jolt to see it and my mind went into a sudden spurt of speed, scrambling frantically to account for it. I had been wrong, it seemed, to think that because the car had been in the road that the house had disappeared. For here was the house exactly as I had seen it just a few hours ago; so it stood to reason that the house had been there all the time and that the car had been moved and I'd been moved as well—a good mile up the road.

It made no sense at all and, furthermore, it seemed impossible. The car had been stuck tight in the ditch. I'd tried to get it out and the wheels had spun and there had been no moving it. And I—drunk as I might have been—certainly could not have been lugged a mile up the road and laid out in a snake den without ever knowing it.

All of it was crazy—the charging Triceratops that had disappeared before it could drive home its charge, the car stuck in the ditch, Snuffy Smith and his wife Lowizey, and even the corn squeezings we had poured down our gullets around the kitchen table. For I had no hangover; I almost wished I had, for if I did I could blame on the fact of being drunk all that was going on. A man couldn't have drunk all the bad moonshine that I remembered drinking and not have felt some sort of repercussions. I had vomited, of course, but that was too late to make any difference so far as a hangover was concerned. By that time the foulness of the booze would have worked its way well throughout my body.

And yet here was what appeared to be the self-same place as I had sought refuge in the night before. True, I had seen it only in the flare of lightning flashes, but it all was there, as I remembered it.

Why the Triceratops, I wondered, and why the rattlesnakes? The dinosaur apparently had been no real danger (it might even have been a hallucination, although I didn't think so), but the rattlesnakes had been for real. They had been a grisly setup for murder and who would want to murder me? And if someone did want to murder me, for reasons which I did not know, surely there would have been easier and less complicated ways in which to go about it.

I was staring at the house so hard that the car almost went off the road. I just barely jerked it back in time.

There had been, to start with, no sign of life about the place, but now, suddenly, there was. Dogs came boiling out of the yard and started racing for the road, bawling at the car. Never in my life had I seen so many dogs, all of them lanky and so skinny that even when they were some distance off, I could see the shine of ribs just underneath their hides. Most of them were hounds, with flapping ears and slender, whiplike tails. Some of them came howling down to the gate and streamed out into the road to head me off and others of them didn't bother with the gate, but sailed across the fence in flying leaps.

The door of the house came open and a man stepped out on the stoop and yelled at them and at his shout they came skidding to a halt, the entire pack of them, and went slinking back toward the house, like a gang of boys caught in a watermelon patch. Those dogs knew very well they had no business chasing cars.

But right at the moment, I wasn't paying too much attention to them, for I was looking at the man who had stepped out to yell at them. I had expected, when he'd stepped out, that he'd be Snuffy Smith. I don't know why I expected this—perhaps because I needed something on which I could hang some logical explanation of what had happened to me. But he wasn't Snuffy Smith. He was considerably taller than Snuffy and he didn't wear a hat and he didn't have a pipe. And I remembered then that the man could not have been Snuffy Smith, for there had been no dogs last night. This was the neighbor that Snuffy had warned me of, the man with the pack of vicious dogs. It would be worth your life, Snuffy had warned me, to go walking down that road.

And it had been damn near worth my life, I reminded myself, to stay with Snuffy Smith, sitting at the kitchen table and drinking moonshine liquor with him.

It was incredible, of course, that I should give credence to the fact that there had been a Snuffy Smith. There wasn't any such person; there simply couldn't be. He and his pinheaded wife were zany characters that paraded through a comic strip. But hard as I tried to tell this to myself, I couldn't make it stick.

Except for the dogs and the man who stood out in the yard yelling at them, the place was the same, however, as Snuffy's place had been. And that, I told myself, was beyond all reason.

Then I saw something that was different and I felt a great deal better about the entire crazy mess, although it was a small thing to feel very good about. There was a car standing by the woodpile, but its rear end wasn't jacked up. It was standing on four wheels, although I saw that a couple of sawhorses and a plank were leaning against the

30

woodpile, as if the car only recently had been jacked up for repair, but that now it had been fixed and taken off the blocks.

I was almost past the place by now and once again the car headed for the ditch and I caught it just in time. When I craned my neck around for a final look, I saw the mailbox that stood on the post beside the gate.

Lettered on it in crude printing, made with a dripping paintbrush, was the name:

T. WILLIAMS

3

George Duncan had grown older, but I recognized him the minute I stepped into the store. He was gray and shaky and he had an old man's gauntness, but he was the same man who had often given me a sack of peppermint candy, free, when my father bought a box of groceries and, perhaps, a sack of bran, which George Duncan lugged in from the back room where he kept his livestock feed.

The storekeeper was behind the counter and talking to a woman who had her back to me. His gravelly voice came clear across the room.

"These Williams kids," he said, "have always been a pack of troublemakers. Ever since the day he came sneaking in here, this community has never had a thing but grief from Tom Williams and his tribe. I tell you, Miss Adams, they're a hopeless lot and if I was you, I wouldn't worry none about them. I'd just go ahead and teach them the best way that I could and I'd crack down on them when they stepped out of line and that would be the end of it."

"But, Mr. Duncan," said the woman, "they aren't all that bad. They have no decent family background, naturally, and sometimes their manners are appalling, but they really aren't vicious. They're under all sorts of pressures—you can't imagine what social pressures they are under . . ."

He grinned at her, a snaggle-toothed grin that had grimness rather than good humor in it. "I know," he said. "I know. You've told me this before, when they were in other scrapes. They're rejected. I think that's what you said."

"That is right," she told him. "Rejected by the other children and rejected by the town. They are left no dignity. When they come in here, I bet you keep an eye on them."

"You are right; I do. They would steal me blind."

"How do you know they would?"

"I've caught them doing it."

"It's resentment," she said. "They are striking back."

"Not at me, they ain't. I never done a thing to them."

"Perhaps not you alone," she said. "Not you personally. But you and everyone. They feel that every hand is raised against them. They know they aren't wanted. They have no place in this community, not because of anything they've done, but because this community decided, long ago, that the family was no good. I think that's the way you say it—the family is no good."

The store, I saw, had changed but little. There were new items on the shelves and there were items that were missing, but the shelves remained the same. The old round glass container that at one time had held a wheel of cheese was gone, but the old tobacco cutter that had been used to slice off squares of chewing tobacco still was bolted to the ledge back of the counter. In one far corner of the store stood a refrigerator case used for dairy goods (which explained, perhaps, the absence of the cheese box on the counter), but that was the only thing that had been really changed in the entire store. The potbellied stove still stood in its pan of sand at the center of the store and the same scarred chairs were ranged about it, polished from long sitting. Up toward the front was the same old pigeonholed compartment of mailboxes with the stamp window in the center of it and from the open door that led into the back came the redolent odor of livestock feed, stacked up in piles of burlap and paper bags.

It was, I thought, as if I'd seen the place only yesterday and had come in this morning to be faintly surprised at the few changes which had been effected overnight.

I turned around and stared out the dirt-streaked, fly-specked window at the street outside and here there were some changes. On the corner opposite the bank a lot, that

I remembered as a vacant lot, now was occupied by a car repair shop thrown up of cement blocks and in front of it a single gas pump with the paint peeled off it. Next door to it was the barber shop, a tiny building that was in no way changed at all except that it seemed somewhat more dingy and in need of paint than I remembered it. And next to it the hardware store, so far as I could see, had not changed at all.

Behind me the conversation apparently had reached its end and I turned around. The woman who had been talking with Duncan was walking toward the door. She was younger than I'd thought when I had seen her talking at the counter. She wore a gray jacket and skirt and her coal-black hair was pulled back tight against her head and knotted in the back. She wore glasses rimmed by some pale plastic and her face had upon it a look of worry and of anger, mixed. She walked with a smart, almost military, gait, and she had the look of a private secretary to a big executive—businesslike and curt and not about to brook any foolishness on the part of anyone.

At the door she turned and asked Duncan, "You're coming to the program tonight, aren't you?"

Duncan grinned with his snaggled teeth. "Haven't missed one yet. Not for many years. Don't reckon I'll start now."

She opened the door then and was swiftly gone. Out of the corner of my eye I watched her marching purposefully down the street.

Duncan came out from behind the counter and shambled toward me.

"Can I do anything for you?" he asked.

"My name is Horton Smith," I said. "I made arrangements . . ."

"Now, just a minute there," said Duncan quickly, peering closely at me. "When your mail started coming in, I recognized the name, but I told myself there must be some mistake. I thought maybe . . ."

"There is no mistake," I said, holding out my hand. "How are you, Mr. Duncan?"

He grasped my hand in a powerful grip and held onto

it. "Little Horton Smith," he said. "You used to come in with your pa . . ."

"And you used to give me a sack of candy."

His eyes twinkled beneath the heavy brows and he gave my hand an extra hearty shake, then dropped it.

It was going to be all right, I told myself. The old Pilot Knob still existed and I was no stranger. I was coming home.

"And you're the same one," he said, "as is on the radio and sometimes on television."

I admitted that I was.

"Pilot Knob," he told me, "is plumb proud of you. It took some getting used to at first to listen to a home-town boy on the radio or sit face to face with him on the television screen. But we got used to it at last and most of us listened to you and talked about it afterwards. We'd go around saying to one another that Horton has said this or that and we took what you had to say for gospel. But," he asked, "what are you doing back? Not that we aren't glad to have you."

"I think I'll stay for a while," I told him. "For a few months, maybe for a year."

"Vacation?"

"No. Not a vacation. There's some writing that I want to do. And to do that writing I had to get away somewhere. Where I would have time for writing and a bit of time for thinking what to write."

"A book?"

"Yes, I hope a book."

"Well, seems to me," he said, rubbing the back of his neck with his hand, "you might have a lot to put into a book. Maybe a lot of things you couldn't say right out on the air. All them foreign places you was in. You were in a lot of them."

"A few of them," I said.

"And Russia? What did you think of Russia?"

"I liked the Russian people. They seemed, in many ways, like us."

"You mean like Americans?"

"Like Americans," I said.

"Well, come over to the stove," he said, "and let us sit and talk. I ain't got a fire in it today. I guess one isn't needed. I can remember, plain as day, your pa sitting in one of these chairs and talking with the others. He was a right good man, your pa, but I always said he wasn't cut out to be a farmer."

We sat down in two of the chairs.

"Is your pa still alive?" he asked.

"Yes, he and Mother both. Out in California. Retired now and very comfortable."

"You got a place to stay?"

I shook my head.

"New motel down by the river," Duncan said. "Built just a year or two ago. New people, by the name of Streeter. Give you good rates if you're staying more than a day or two. I'll make sure they do it. I'll speak to them about it."

"There's no need . . ."

"But you ain't no transient. You're home folk, come back again. They would want to know."

"Any fishing?"

"Best place on the river. Got some boats to rent and a canoe or two, although why anyone would risk their neck in a canoe on that river is more than I can figure."

"I was hoping for a place like that," I said. "I was afraid there would be none."

"Still crazy about fishing?"

"I enjoy it," I said.

"Remember when you were a boy you were rough on chubs."

"Chubs made good fun," I said.

"There're still a lot of people you will remember," said Duncan. "They'll all want to see you. Why don't you drop in on the school program tonight? A lot of people will be there. That was the teacher that was in here, name of Kathy Adams."

"You still have the old one-room school?"

"You can bet we have," he said. "There was pressure put on us and some of the other districts to consolidate, but when it was put up to a vote we beat it. Kids get just

37

as good an education in a one-room school as they would get in a new and fancy building and it costs a whole lot less. Kids that want to go to high school, we pay their tuition, but there aren't many of them that want to go. Still costs less than if we were consolidated. No use spending money for a high school when you got a bunch of kids like them Williams brats . . ."

"I am sorry," I said, "but when I stepped inside I couldn't help but hear . . ."

"Let me tell you, Horton, that Kathy Adams is a splendid teacher, but she is too soft-hearted. She is always standing up for them Williams kids and I tell you they are nothing but a gang of cutthroats. I guess you don't know Tom Williams; he came floating in here after you had left. He worked around on some of the farms, but he was mostly good-for-nothing, although he must have managed to save a little money. He was well past marrying age when he got hitched up with one of Little Poison Carter's daughters. Amelia was her name. You remember Little Poison, don't you?"

I shook my head.

"Had a brother that was called Big Poison. No one now recollects their rightful names. The whole tribe lived down on Muskrat Island. Well, anyhow, when Tom married Amelia he bought, with the money he had saved, this little shirttail piece of land a couple of miles up Lonesome Hollow and tried to make a farm of it. He's got along somehow; I wouldn't know exactly how. And every year or so there was a kid and him and Mrs. Tom let those kids run wild. I tell you, Horton, these are the kind of folks we can get along without. They cause no end of trouble—Old Tom Williams and that family that he's raising. They keep more dogs than you can shake a stick at and those dogs are worthless, just like Old Tom himself. They lay around all day and they eat their heads off and they ain't worth a lick. Tom says he just likes dogs. Have you ever heard a thing like that? A trifling kind of fellow, with his dogs and kids and the kids are always in some kind of trouble."

"Miss Adams seemed to think," I reminded him, "that it's not their fault entirely."

"I know. She says they felt rejected and are underprivileged. That's another favorite word of hers. You know what underprivileged means? It means someone who has no get-up-and-go. There wouldn't need to be no underprivileged if everyone was willing to work and had a lick of common sense. Oh, I know what the government says about them and how we got to help them. But if the government just would come out here and have a look at some of these underprivileged folks, they'd see in a minute what was wrong with them."

"I was wondering," I said, "as I drove along this morning, if there still are rattlesnakes."

"Rattlesnakes?" he asked.

"There used to be a lot of them when I was a kid. I was wondering if they might be getting thinned out some."

He wagged his head sagaciously. "Maybe some. Although there's still a bait of them. Get back in the hills and you'll find plenty of them. You interested in them?"

"Not especially," I said.

"You'll have to come to that school program tonight," he said. "There'll be a lot of people there. Some of them you'll know. Last day of school and the kids will all perform—get up and say some pieces or maybe sing a song or put on little plays. And afterwards there'll be a basket social to raise money for new library books. We still hang on to the old ways here; the years haven't changed us much. And we manage to have our own good times. A basket social at the school tonight and a couple of weeks from now there'll be a strawberry festival down at the Methodist church. Both of them good places to meet old friends of yours."

"I'll make it if I can," I promised. "Both the program and the festival."

"You've got some mail," he told me. "It has been piling up for a week or two. I still am postmaster here. The post office has been right here in this store for almost a hundred years. But there's talk of taking it away from us, consolidating it with the office over at Lancaster and sending it out from there by rural route. Government isn't satisfied leaving things alone. They got to always be trying to make

39

things over. Improving service, they call it. I can't see, for the life of me, what's wrong with the kind of service we been giving the folks of Pilot Knob for the last hundred years or so."

"I had expected you might have a bundle of mail for me," I said. "I had it forwarded, but I didn't hurry to get here. I took my time and stopped at several places I wanted to look over."

"You'll be going out to have a look at the old farm, the place you used to live?"

"I don't think I will," I said. "I'd see too many changes."

"Family by the name of Ballard lives there now," he said. "They have a couple of boys, grown men almost. Do a lot of drinking, those two boys, and sometimes are a problem."

I nodded. "You say this motel is down by the river?"

"That's right. You drive down past the schoolhouse and the church to where the road bends to the left. A little ways beyond you will see the sign. Says River Edge Motel. I'll get your mail for you."

4

The large manila envelope had Philip Freeman's return address written in a scrawling hand across its upper left-hand corner. I sat in the chair by the open window, turning it slowly in my hand, wondering why Philip should be writing or sending anything to me. I knew the man, of course, and liked him, but we never had been close. The only link between us was our mutual affection and respect for the grand old man who had died some weeks before in an auto accident.

Through the window came the talking of the river, the muttered conversation it held with the countryside as it went sliding through the land. The sound of its talk, as I sat there listening, brought back in memory the times when my father and I had sat on its bank and fished—always with my father, but never by myself. For the river potentially was too dangerous for a boy of ten. The creek, of course, was all right if I promised to be careful.

The creek had been a friend, a shining summer friend, but the river had been magic. And it was magic still, I thought, a magic compounded of boyhood dreams and time. And finally here I was again beside it; here I would live beside it for a time and now I realized that I was afraid, deep inside myself, that living close beside it I would get to know it so well that the magic would be lost and it would become just another river running down another land.

Here were quiet and peace, I thought—the kind of quiet and peace that could be found in only a few other backwater corners of the earth. Here a man might find the time and space to think, undisturbed by the intrusion of the static that was given off by the rumblings of world commerce and global politics. Here was a country that the rush of progress had swept past, barely touching it.

Barely touching it, and thus leaving it with some of its old ideas. This place did not know that God was dead; in the little church at the upper end of the village the minister still might preach of fire and brimstone and his congregation would give him rapt attention. This place felt no overwhelming social guilt; it still believed that it was meet and proper that a man should work to earn a living. This place did not subscribe to deficit spending; it tried to get along with what it had and thus hold down the taxes. Once good and sterling virtues, but no longer so if measured against modern attitudes. And yet, I thought, not buried in the trivia of the outside world—escaping not only the physical trivia, but the intellectual and the moral and the aesthetic trivia as well. Still able to believe, in a world that had stopped believing. Still holding fast to certain values, even if mistaken values, in a world that had few values left. Still fiercely concerned about the fundamentals of life and living while much of the world long since had escaped into cynicism.

I glanced about the room, a simple place—small and bright and clean, with a minimum of furniture, with paneling on the wall and no carpet on the floor. A monk's cell, I thought, and that was the way it should be, for a man could do little work smothered in an overburden of conveniences.

Peace and quiet, I thought, and what about the rattlesnakes? Could this peace and quiet be no more than a tricky surface, the millpond water that masked a whirlpool's violence? I saw it all again—the cruel, skull-like head hanging over me—and as I remembered it my body ached with a recall of the tension that had frozen it into immobility.

Why should anyone have planned and executed such a bizarre attempt at murder? Who had done it and how had it been carried out and why should it be me? Why had

42

there been two farmhouses so alike that one could scarcely be differentiated from the other? And what about Snuffy Smith and the stuck car that wasn't really stuck and the Triceratops that after a little time wasn't there at all?

I gave up. There were no answers. The only possible answer seemed to be that it had never happened and I was sure it had. A man could imagine any one of all these things, perhaps; he could not, certainly, imagine all of them. There must, I knew, be an explanation somewhere, but I didn't have it.

I laid the manila envelope aside and looked at the other mail and there was little of importance. There were several notes from friends wishing me well in my new place of residence, but most of the notes had a trace of false joviality about them I was not sure I liked. Everyone, it seemed, thought that I was slightly crazy to bury myself in what to them was wilderness to write what probably would turn out to be a very lousy book. There were a couple of bills I had forgotten to pay and there were a magazine or two and some advertising.

I picked up the manila envelope again and ripped it open. Out of it came a sheaf of Xeroxed pages with a handwritten note clipped to them.

The note said:

Dear Horton: When I went through the papers in Uncle's desk, I ran across the enclosed and, knowing you were one of his closest and most valued friends, I ran off a copy for you. Frankly, I don't know what to make of it. With some other man I might think it was nothing more than a fantasy that, for some whimsical, personal reason, he had written down—perhaps to clear it from his mind. But Uncle was not whimsical, as I think you will agree. I am wondering if he might at some time have mentioned this to you. If such should be the case, you may have a better understanding of it than I seem able to muster — Philip.

43

I pulled the note clear from the stapled Xeroxed sheets and there, in the crabbed, miserly handwriting of my friend (a handwriting so unlike the man himself), was the document.

There was no heading on the sheet. Nothing to tell what he had intended it to be.

I settled down into the chair and began to read.

5

The evolutionary process (the document began) is a phenomenon which has been of special and absorbing interest to me all my life, although in my own particular field I have been concerned only with one small, and perhaps unspectacular, aspect of it. As a professor of history, I have been more and more intrigued, as the years go on, with the evolutionary trend of human thought. I would be ashamed to enumerate how many times I've tried and how many hours I've spent in attempting to draw up a graph or chart or diagram, or whatever one might call it, to show the change and development in human thought through all historic ages. The subject, however, is too vast and too diverse (and in some instances, I might as well confess, too contradictory) to lend itself to any illustrative scheme I've been able to devise. And yet I am sure that human thought has been evolutionary, that the basis of it has shifted steadily through all of man's recorded time, that we do not think as we did a hundred years ago, that our opinions are much changed from a thousand years ago, not so much attributable to the fact that we now have better knowledge upon which to base our thinking, but that the human viewpoint has undergone a change—an evolution, if you please.

It may seem amusing that anyone should become so absorbed in the process of human thought. But those who think it amusing would be wrong. For it is the capability of abstract thought and nothing else which distinguishes the human being from any other creature that lives upon the earth.

Let us take a look at evolution, without attempting, or pretending to delve deeply into it, only touching a few of those more obvious landmarks which we are told by paleontologists highlight the path of progress from that primal ocean in which the first microscopic forms of life came into being at a very distant time. Not hunting for, or concerning ourselves with all the subtle changes which marked development, but only noting some of the horizon lines which stand out as a result of all those subtle changes.

One of those first great landmarks must necessarily be the emergence of certain life forms from the water to live upon the land. This ability to change environment undoubtedly was a much protracted and perhaps a painful and probably a hazardous procedure. But to us today time telescopes it into a single event which stands out as a high point in the evolutionary scheme. Another high point was the development of the notochord which, in millions of years to come, evolved into a backbone. Yet another high point was the development of bipedal locomotion, although I, personally, am inclined to discount somewhat the significance of the erect position. If one talks of man, it was not the ability to walk erect, but the ability to think beyond the moment and in other terms than the here and now that made him what he is today.

The evolutionary process represents a long chain of events. Many evolutionary trends ran their courses and were discarded and many species became extinct because they were tied inexorably into some of those evolutionary trends. But it was always from some factor, or perhaps from many factors which were involved in the development of those extinct life forms, that new evolutionary lines arose. And the thought must occur to one that through all this tangled jungle of change and modification there must have run a single central core of evolution pointing toward some final form. Through all the millions of years, that central evolutionary form, now expressed in man, lay in the slow growth of a brain which in time became a mind.

One thing, it seems to me, that stands out in the evolutionary process is that while developments, once they've happened, do make uncommon sense, no observer before the fact could have made a valid prediction that they were about to happen. It would not have made good sense for an observer, a half billion years ago, to have predicted that in a few more million years life forms would leave the water and live upon the land. It would have seemed, as a matter of fact, a most unlikely thing, well-nigh impossible. For life forms as they were then constructed, needed the water; they could live nowhere else but in the water. And the land of that day, sterile and barren, must have seemed as incredibly hostile to life as space seems to us today.

Life forms, half a billion years ago, were small. Smallness then must have seemed as much a part of life as water. No observer in that day could possibly have imagined the monster dinosaurs of later ages, or the modern whale. Such size the observer would have thought to be impossible. Flying he would not have thought of at all; it would have been a concept which would not have crossed his mind. And even if, by some remote chance, it had, he would have seen no way for it to happen, or no reason for it.

So while we can look back, after the fact, and sense the validity and the rightness of all evolutionary progress, there seems no way in which it can be predicted.

The question of what may come after man is a thought which has arisen at times, although largely as a matter of idle speculation. There is a reluctance, I would imagine, for anyone to think too seriously of it. Most people would believe, if they thought of it at all, that it is a question which lies so far in the future that it is senseless for one to give it consideration. The primates have been around only eighty million years or so, perhaps somewhat less than that; man for only two or three million, even at the most optimistic calculation. So, measured against the trilobites and dinosaurs, the primates have many millions of years still left before they become extinct or before they lose their position of dominance upon the earth.

Also there may be a reluctance to admit, even by the thinking of it, that man ever will become extinct. Some men (by no means all of them) can reconcile themselves to the realization that they, personally, some day will die. A man can imagine the world with himself no longer in it; it is far more difficult to imagine an earth with no humans left. We shy away, with some strange inner fear, from the death of the species. We know, intellectually, if not emotionally, that some day we, as members of the human race, will cease to exist; it is difficult to think, however, that the human race itself is not immortal and eternal. We can say that man is the only species which has developed the means by which he can bring about his own extinction. But while we may say this, we do not, in our hearts, believe it.

What little serious speculation there has been about this subject has not really been about it at all. There seems to be a mental block which prevents consideration of it. We almost never speculate upon what might supersede man; what we do is to conjure up a future superman—inhuman in many ways, perhaps, but still a man. Alienated from us in a mental and intellectual sense, but still, biologically, a man. Even here, in this kind of speculation, we perpetuate the stubborn belief that man will go on forever and forever.

This, of course, is wrong. Unless the evolutionary process, in bringing forth the human race, has reached a dead end, there will be something more than man. History would seem to say that the evolutionary process has not reached a dead end. Through the ages there has been evidence that the principle of evolution is never at a loss to produce new life forms or to introduce new survival values. There is no reason to believe, on present evidence, that in man the evolutionary process has used up all its bag of tricks.

So there will be something after man, something other than man. Not just an extension or modification of man,

48

but something entirely different. We ask, in horror and disbelief, what could supersede man, what could beat intelligence?

I believe I know.

I believe the superseder is already in existence and has been for many years.

Abstract thought is a new thing in the world. No other creature than man ever has been blessed (or cursed) with such a faculty. It took from us the old security accorded other creatures which are aware of nothing except the here and now, and in some cases aware only dimly of the here and now. It let us look into the past and, what is worse, peer darkly futureward. It made us aware of loneliness, and filled us with a hope, from which stemmed hopelessness, and it showed us how we stood alone, naked and defenseless, before the uncaring of the cosmos. That day when the first manlike creature became aware of the implications of space and time as related to himself must be classed, at once, as the most fearful and most glorious day in the history of life upon the earth.

We used our intelligence for many practical purposes and for theoretical probing which, in turn, gave us other answers for practical application. And we used it for something else as well. We used it to fill an enigmatic world with many shadowy creatures—with gods, devils, angels, ghosts, nymphs, fairies, brownies, goblins. We created in our tribal minds a dark and warring world in which we had enemies and allies. And we created other mythical creatures which were neither dark nor fearsome, but simply pleasant products of our imagination—Santa Claus, the Easter Rabbit, Jack Frost, the Sandman, and many, many others. Not only did we create these things intellectually, but we believed in them in varying degrees. We saw them and we talked of them and they were very real to us. Why, if not for fear of meeting such things, did the peasants of medieval days in Europe bar their hovels at the fall of night and refuse to venture out? Why the fear of the dark still inherent in many modern men if it is not the fear of meeting something in the dark? Today we talk but little of these things of the dark, but that the old uneasiness and fear may still be with us is demonstrated by the wide belief today in such things as flying saucers. In this enlightened day it may be childish to talk of werewolf or of ghoul, but it is all right to believe in a technical wraith such as a flying saucer.

What do we know of abstract thought? The answer, of course, is that we know nothing of it. There is a possibility, I understand, that it may be electrical in nature and that it is based upon some sort of energy exchange, for the physicists tell us that all processes must be based on energy. But what do we know, actually, either of electricity or of energy? What do we know, when one comes down to it, about anything at all? Do we know how the atom works or why it works or what an atom is? Can anyone explain the awareness of self and environment which distinguishes life from inorganic matter?

We think of thought as a mental process and we do lip service to the physicists by admitting that an energy exchange must somehow be involved. But we know no more about the thought processes, perhaps even less, than the ancient Greeks knew about the atom. Democritus, who lived during the fourth century before Christ, is generally accorded the honor of being the first man to put forward the atomic theory, and this was, admittedly, an advance in thinking, but the atoms of Democritus were a far cry, indeed, from what we now think of as atoms—and, which, incidentally, we still do not understand. So we talk of thought today as the Greeks in the day of Democritus may have talked (although only briefly and without too much conviction or belief) about the atom, and with as little understanding. We are, when it comes down to the truth of it, only mouthing words.

We do know something of the result of thought. All that mankind has today is the product of his thinking. But this is the result of the impact of the thought upon the human animal, as steam makes an impact upon a mechanism and makes an engine run.

We might ask, once the steam has made its impact and performed its function, what happens to the steam? I think that it is as logical to ask, once thought has made its impact, what happens to the thought—to that exchange of energy which we are told is necessary to bring about and produce the thought.

I think I know the answer. I believe that thought, the energy of thought, whatever strange form thought itself might take, streaming unceasingly through the centuries from the minds of billions of men and women, has given rise to a group of beings which in time, perhaps a not too distant time, will supersede the human race.

Thus the superseding species arises from that very mechanism, the mind, which has made mankind the dominant species of today. This, as I read the record, is the way that evolution works.

Man has built with his hands, but he builds with mind as well, and I believe better and somewhat differently than he might imagine.

One man's thought about a vicious, ghoulish shape lurking in the dark would not bring that lurking shape into actual being. But an entire tribe, all thinking (and afraid) of this same ghoulish shape would bring it, I believe, into actual being. The shape was not there to start with. It existed only in the mind of one man, crouching frightened in the dark. And frightened of he knew not what, he felt he must give shape to this thing of fear and so he imagined it and told the others what he had imagined and they imagined it as well. And they imagined it so long and well and so believed in it that eventually they created it.

Evolution works in many ways. It works in any way it can. That it had never operated in quite this way before may merely have been because until the human mind developed it never possessed an agency which would allow it to bring about actual entities out of the sheer force of imagination. And not out of imagination alone, not by wishful thinking, but out of the forces and energies which man as yet does not understand and may never understand.

I believe that man, with his imagination, with his love of story telling, with his fear of time and space, of death and dark, working through millenia, has created another

51

world of creatures which share the earth with him—hidden, invisible, I do not know, but I am sure that they are here and that some day they may come out from their concealment and enter upon their heritage.

Scattered throughout the literature of the world and through the daily flow of news events are strange happenings too well documented to be mere illusions in each and every case . . .

6

The writing ended in the middle of the page, but there were many other pages and when I flipped the sheet over I saw that the next page was crammed with a jumble of what appeared to be a mass of notes. Written in the crabbed calligraphy of my friend, they were jammed into the page as if the sheet of paper had been the only one he'd had and he had schemed and planned to use every inch of it to cram in his fact and observation. The notes marched in a solid phalanx down the center of the page and then the margins of the page were filled with further notes and some of the writing was so pinched and small that there would have been difficulty, in many instances, in making out the words.

I riffled through the other pages and each one was the same, filled and crammed with notes.

I flipped the pages back and clipped the note from Philip onto the front of the sheaf of pages.

Later, I told myself, I would read the notes—read them and attempt to puzzle through them. But for the moment I had read enough, far more than enough.

It was a joke, I thought—but it could not be a joke, for my old friend never joked. He did not need to joke. He was filled with gentleness and he was vastly erudite and when he talked he had more use for words than to employ them in telling stupid jokes.

And I remembered him again as he had been that last time I had seen him, sitting like a shrunken gnome in the great lounge chair which threatened to engulf him, and how he said to me, "I think that we are haunted." He had been about to tell me something that night, I was convinced, but he had not told it, for when he'd been about to tell it Philip had come in and we'd talked of something else.

I felt sure, sitting there in the motel room by the river, that he had meant to tell me what I had just read—that we are haunted by all the creatures that man has ever dreamed of, that mankind's mind has served an evolutionary function through its imagination.

He was wrong, of course. On the face of it, his belief encompassed an impossibility. But even as I thought that he must be wrong, I knew deep inside myself that no man such as he could be lightly wrong. Before he had committed to paper what he had, if for no other reason than to outline his thinking for himself, he had arrived at his conclusions only after long and thoughtful study. Those pages of appended notes were not, I was certain, the only evidence he had. Rather they would be the condensation and the summary of all the evidence he'd gathered, all the thinking he had done. He still could be wrong, of course, and very likely was, but still with enough evidence and logic that his idea could not be summarily dismissed.

He had meant to tell me, to test out his theory on me, perhaps. But because of Philip's showing up, he had put it off. And it was then too late, for in a day or two he'd died, his car crumpled up and the life smashed out of him by an impact with another car that had not been found.

Thinking of it, I felt myself growing cold with a terrible kind of fear, a new kind of fear I'd never felt before—a fear that crept out of another world than this, that came from some far corner of an old ancestral mind many times removed, the cold, numbing, gut-squeezing fear of a man who crouched inside a cave and listened to the sound made by the ghoulish shape that was prowling in the outer dark.

Could it be, I asked myself, could it be that the mind-force of this other world of prowling things has reached such a point of development and efficiency that it could assume any shape at all, a shape for any purpose? Could it become a car that smashed another car and, having smashed it, return to that other world or dimension or invisibility from which it had emerged?

Had my old friend died because he had guessed the secret of this other world of mind-created things?

And the rattlesnakes, I wondered. No, not the rattlesnakes, for I was sure that they had been real. But had the Triceratops, the house and the other buildings, the jacked-up car beside the woodpile, Snuffy Smith and his wife not been real? Was this the answer that I needed? Could all of these things have been made up of a masquerading mind-force that lay in ambush for me, that fooled me into accepting the improbable even when I had felt it was all improbable, that had escorted me, not to the couch in the living room, but to the rocky floor of a snake-infested cave?

And if so, why? Because this hypothetical mind-force knew that the manila envelope from Philip awaited my arrival at George Duncan's store?

It was insanity, I told myself. But so had missing the turn in the road been insanity, so had been the Triceratops, so had been the house where there was no house, so had been the rattlesnakes. But not the snakes, I said, for the snakes were real. And what was real? I asked. How could one know that anything was real? At this late day, if my old friend had been right, was anything for real?

I was shaken deeper than I knew. I sat in the chair and stared at the wall, and the sheaf of papers fell from my hand and I did not move to pick them up. If this were so, I thought, our old and trustworthy world had been jerked from beneath our feet, and the goblins and the ghouls were no longer something for mere chimney-corner tales, but existed in the very solid flesh—well, not perhaps in solid flesh, but they anyhow existed; they were not illusions. A product of imagination, we had said of them, and we had been entirely right without our knowing it. And again, if this were so, Nature, in the process of evolution, had made a long, long jump ahead, from living matter to intelligence and from intelligence to abstract thought and from abstract thought to some form of life at once shadowy and real, a life, perhaps, that could take its choice of being either shadowy or real.

I tried to imagine what sort of life it might be, what might be its joys and its sorrows, what could be its motives; I could not imagine any of it. My blood and bone and flesh would not allow me to. For it would have to be another form of life and the gap was much too great. As well, or better, to ask a trilobite to imagine the world of the dinosaurs. If Nature were seeking for survival values in its continual winnowing of species, here finally it should have found a creature (if it could be called a creature) with a fantastically high survival value, for there would be nothing, absolutely nothing, in the physical world that could get at it.

I sat there, thinking of it, and the thoughts bounced in my skull like the mutterings of distant thunder and I was getting nowhere in my thinking. I wasn't even going around in circles. I was just bouncing back and forth, like a half-demented Yo-Yo.

With an effort I jerked myself out of all this crazy thinking and once again I heard the gurgle and the laughter and the chuckling of the river as it went running down the land in the splendor of its magic.

There was unpacking to be done, getting all the bags and boxes out of the car and hauled into the room; there was fishing waiting for me, with the canoe at the dock and the big bass lurking in the reeds and among the lily pads. And after that, getting settled down, a book that must be written.

And there was, as well, I recalled, the program and the basket social at the school tonight. I would have to be there.

7

Linda Bailey spotted me as soon as I walked through the school house door and came bustling over to me like a self-important hen. She was one of the few people there that I remembered and there was no way one could fail to remember her. She and her husband and her brood of grubby children had lived on the farm next door to ours and there had been few days during the entire time that we were there that Linda Bailey had not come traipsing up the road or across the fields to borrow a cup of sugar or a dab of butter or any one of a dozen other items of which she continually found herself short and which, incidentally, she never seemed to get around to paying back. She was a large, raw-boned, horsey woman and she had aged, it seemed to me, but little.

"Horace Smith!" she trumpeted. "Little Horace Smith. I'd knowed you anywhere."

She flung her arms about me and she pounded me on the back with resounding thumps while, embarrassed, I struggled to remember just what bond of affection there had been between my family and the Bailey family to justify this kind of greeting.

"So you came back again," she yelped. "You couldn't stay away. Once Pilot Knob gets into your blood, there can't no one stay away. And after being to all those places, too. To all them heathen countries. You were in Rome, weren't you?"

"I spent some time in Rome," I told her. "It's not a heathen country."

"The purple iris that I have down against the pigpen,"

she declared, "is from the Pope's own garden. It's not so much to look at. I've seen lots better iris—a whole lot prettier. Any other kind of iris no better than that I'd dug up and throwed out long ago. But I kept it because of the place it come from. It ain't everybody, I can tell you, that has iris from the Pope's own garden. Not that I hold with the Pope and all that foolishness, but it does make the iris sort of distinctive, don't you think it does?"

"Very much," I said.

She grabbed me by the arm. "For goodness' sake," she said, "let's go over and sit down. We have so much to talk about."

She dragged me to a row of chairs and we sat down together.

"You said Rome wasn't no heathen country," she said, "but you been in heathen countries. What about them Russians? You spent a lot of time in Russia."

"I don't know," I said. "Some of the Russian people still believe in God. It's the government . . ."

"Land sakes alive," she said, "you sound as if you liked them Russians."

"Some of them," I said.

"I heard," she said, "that you were up Lonesome Hollow and came driving down the road past the Williams place this morning. What in the world would you be doing there?"

Was there anything, I wondered, that she didn't know about, that all Pilot Knob didn't know about? Better than tribal drums, more efficient than radio, the news went thrumming through the community—every bit of gossip, every supposition.

"I turned up the road on impulse," I told her, lying very feebly. "When I was a boy, I went squirrel hunting up there sometimes in the fall."

She looked at me suspiciously, but she didn't follow up the reason for my being there. "Maybe it's all right in daylight," she declared, "but I wouldn't, for all the money in the world, go up there after dark." She leaned closer to me and her braying voice sank to a scratchy whisper.

"The place is haunted," she said, "by a pack of dogs, if you want to call them dogs. They come baying down across the hills, snarling and yapping, and when they go past there is a cold wind going with them. It's enough to freeze your soul . . ."

"You've heard these dogs?" I asked.

"Heared them? On many a night I've heared them, howling down the hills, but I've never been that close to them that I've felt the wind. Nettie Campbell told me. You remember Nettie Campbell?"

I shook my head.

"Oh, of course you wouldn't. She was Nettie Graham before she married Andy Campbell. They lived at the end of the road up Lonesome Hollow. The house is deserted now. Just walked away and left. Them dogs drove them off. Maybe you saw it—saw the house, I mean."

I nodded, not too positively, for I'd not seen the house. I'd only heard of it from Lowizie Smith the night before.

"There are strange things in these hills," said Linda Bailey. "Things a body, in his right mind, would not believe. It comes, I suppose, from being such wild country. A lot of other places are all settled down, with not a tree left standing and all the land in fields. But this is still wild country. I guess it will always be."

The schoolroom was beginning to fill up now and I saw George Duncan making his way through the crowd toward me. I stood up to greet him and held out my hand.

"I hear you got settled in all right," he said. "I knew you'd like the place. I phoned Streeter and told him to look after you. He said you were out fishing. Catch anything worthwhile?"

"A couple of bass," I told him. "I'll do better once I get to know the river."

"I think the program is about to start," he said. "I'll see you later on. There are a lot of people here you should say hello to."

The program got underway. The teacher, Kathy Adams, played the old delapidated organ and different groups of kids came up and sang some songs and others

59

spoke their pieces and a bunch of eighth grade pupils put on a little play that Kathy Adams proudly announced they had worked out themselves.

It all, in its stumbling way, was entirely delightful and I sat there remembering when I had gone to school in this very building and had taken part in exactly such a program. I tried to remember the names of some of the teachers I had had and it was only toward the end of the program that I remembered one of them had been named Miss Stein, a strange, angular, flighty person with an abundance of red hair and most easily upset by some of the pranks we were always thinking up. I wondered where Miss Stein might be this very evening and how life had treated her. Better, I hoped, than some of us kids had treated her when we had gone to school.

Linda Bailey tugged at my jacket sleeve and spoke in a grating whisper. "Them kids are good, ain't they?"

I nodded that they were.

"This Miss Adams is a right good teacher," Linda Bailey whispered. "I'm afraid that she won't stay here long. This little school of ours can't expect to keep someone as good as her."

Then the program was over and George Duncan came pushing through the crowd and took me in tow and began to introduce me to some other people. Some of them I remembered and some of them I didn't, but they seemed to remember me, so I pretended that I did.

But right in the middle of it Miss Adams was standing up on the little platform at the front of the room and calling to George Duncan, "You forgot," she told him, "or are you pretending to, in hopes you'll get out of it? But you promised to be our auctioneer tonight."

George protested, but I could see that he was pleased. One could see with only half an eye that George Duncan was an important person in Pilot Knob. He owned the general store and was the postmaster and a member of the school board and he could turn his hand to many other little civic chores, like auctioneering the baskets at a basket social. He was the man that Pilot Knob always turned to when they needed something done.

So he went up to the platform and turned to the table that was stacked with decorated baskets and boxes and picked one of them up for the crowd to look at. But before he started in on his auctioneering, he made a little speech.

"All of you know," he said, "what this is all about. The proceeds from this basket social will be used to buy new books for the school library, so you will have the satisfaction of knowing that whatever you spend here will be used to a good purpose. You aren't just buying the basket and the privilege of eating with the lady whose name you find inside it; you also are contributing to a very praiseworthy public cause. So I'll ask you fellows out there to loosen up a bit and spend some of that money that is sagging down your pockets."

He hoisted the basket that he held. "Now here," he said, "is the kind of basket that I like to offer. I tell you, fellows, this one has a hefty feel to it. There's a lot of good eating packed into it and the way it's decorated and all, I'd say the lady who put it up probably paid as much attention to what went into it as how it looks outside. And it might interest you to know that I seem to catch a whiff of good fried chicken."

"Now," he asked, "what am I bid?"

"A dollar," said someone, and someone else immediately made it two and then from the back of the room came a bid of two and a half.

"Two dollars and a half," said George Duncan in aggrieved surprise. "Are you boys going to stop at two and a half? Why, if you were to buy this basket by the pound, that would be dirt cheap. Now do I hear . . ."

Someone bid three dollars and George worked it up from there, fifty cents and a quarter at a time, to four seventy-five and finally knocked it down for that.

I looked about the crowd. They were a group of friendly folks and they were having a good time. They were spending an evening with their neighbors and were comfortable with them. Right now they were intent upon the selling of the baskets, but later on there would be time for talk and there would be little weighty talk, I knew. They'd talk about the crops, the fishing, the new road that had been talked about for twenty years or more but had never come about and now was being talked about again, of the latest scandal (for there always was a scandal of some sort, although often of the very mildest kind), of the sermon the minister had preached last Sunday, of the old gentleman very newly dead and beloved by all of them. They'd talk of many things and then they'd go home through the softness of the late spring evening and they'd have their little worries and their neighborhood concerns, but there would be none of them weighed down by huge official worries. And it was good, I told myself, to be in a place where there were no overpowering and dark official worries.

I felt someone tugging at my sleeve and looked in the direction of the tugging and there was Linda Bailey.

"You'd ought to bid on that one," she whispered at me. "That one belongs to the preacher's daughter. She's a pretty thing. You'd enjoy meeting her."

"How do you know," I asked, "that it's the preacher's daughter's basket?"

"I just know," she said. "Go ahead and bid."

It was up to three dollars and I said three dollars and a half and immediately, from across the room, came a bid for four. I looked where the bid had come from and there, standing, ranged with their backs against the wall, were three young men, in their early twenties. When I looked at them I found that all three were looking at me and it seemed to me that they were sneering at me in a very heavy-handed way.

The tug came at my sleeve again. "Go ahead and bid," urged Linda Bailey. "It's them Ballard boys and the other one's a Williams. They are terrible louts. Nancy will just die if any of the three of them should bid in her basket."

"Four fifty," I said, unthinking, and up on the platform George Duncan said, "I have four fifty. Who will make it five?" He turned toward the three ranged along the wall and one of them said five. "Now I have five," sang George. "Will someone make it six?" He was looking straight at me and I shook my head, so he sold it for the five.

"Why did you do that?" Linda Bailey raged at me in her neighing whisper. "You could have kept on bidding."

"Not on your life," I told her. "I'm not going to come into this town and the first night I am here make it tough for some young sprout to buy the basket that he wants. His girl might be involved. She might have told him beforehand how to identify her basket."

"But Nancy's not his girl," said Linda Bailey, much disgusted at me. "Nancy hasn't got a fellow. She'll be mortified."

"You said that they were Ballards. Aren't they the people who live on our old home farm?"

"That they are," she said. "And the old folks are nice enough. But them two boys of theirs! They are holy terrors. All the girls are scared of them. They go to dances all the time and they are filthy-mouthed and do a lot of drinking."

I looked across the room and the three still were watching me, with triumphant leers pasted on their faces. I was a stranger to the town and they had bluffed me out, they had overbid me. It was silly on the face of it, of course, but in a little place like this small triumphs and small insults, because of the lack of any other kind, are often magnified.

Christ, I thought, why did I have to run into this Bailey woman? She'd always been bad news and she hadn't changed. She was a meddler and a busybody and there was no good in her.

The baskets were going rapidly and only a few of them were left. George was getting tired and the bidding had slowed down. I told myself that perhaps I should buy a basket, to demonstrate, if nothing else, that I was no stranger, but was a man, instead, who had come back to Pilot Knob and meant to stay awhile.

I looked around and there was no sign of Linda Bailey. More than likely she was sore at me and had stalked away. Thinking of her, I felt a little flare of anger. What right had she to demand that I protect the minister's daughter, Nancy, against the more than likely innocent designs—or at least ineffectual, if not innocent designs—of some loutish farm boy.

There were only three baskets left now and George picked up one of them. It was only half the size some of the others had been and it was not overdecorated. Holding it up, he began his auction singsong.

There were two or three bids and they got it up to three fifty and I made it four.

Someone over against the wall said five and I glanced in that direction and the three were grinning at me—grinning, it seemed to me, with all the clownish malice in the world.

"Make it six," I said.

"Seven," said the middle one of the trio.

"I have seven," said George, somewhat aghast, for this was the highest any bid had run that night. "Do I hear seven and a half or does someone want to make it eight?"

I hesitated for a moment. I was certain that the first few bids had not come from any of the three against the wall. They had only entered the bidding after I had made my bid. They were, I was certain, deliberately baiting me and I was sure, as well, that everyone in the room knew what they were up to.

"Eight?" asked George, still looking at me. "Do I hear an eight?"

"Not eight," I told him. "Let us make it ten."

George gulped. "Ten!" he cried. "Do I hear eleven?"

He switched his eyes to the three against the wall. They glared back at him.

"Eleven," he said. "It takes eleven. No raise smaller than a dollar. Do I hear eleven?"

He didn't hear eleven.

When I went to the front of the room to pay the auction clerk and to get the basket, I glanced at the wall. The three were no longer there.

Standing to one side, I opened the basket and the name on the slip of paper placed atop the lunch was that of Kathy Adams.

8

The first lilacs were coming out and in the cool, damp evening they had filled the air with a faint suggestion of that fragrance which, in the weeks to come, would hang a heavy perfume along all the streets and footpaths of this little town. A wind, blowing up the hollow from the river, set the suspended street lights at the intersections swinging and the light and shadow on the ground went bouncing back and forth.

"I'm glad that it is over," Kathy Adams said. "The program, I mean, and the school year too. But I'll be coming back in September."

I looked down at the girl walking at my side and she was, it seemed to me, an entirely different person than the one I'd seen that morning in the store. She had done something to her hair and the schoolteacherish look of it was gone and she'd put away her glasses. Protective coloration, I wondered—the way she'd looked that morning, a deliberate effort to make herself appear the kind of teacher who would gain acceptance in this community. And it was a shame, I told myself. Given half a chance, she was a pretty girl.

"You said you'll be back," I said. "Where will you spend the summer?"

"Gettysburg," she said.

"Gettysburg?"

"Gettysburg, P.A.," she told me. "I was born there and my family still is there. I go back each summer."

"I was there just a few days ago," I said. "I stopped on my way here. Spent two full days, wandering the battlefield and wondering what it had all been like that time more than a hundred years ago."

"You'd never been there before?"

"Once before. Many years ago. When I first went to Washington as a cub reporter. I took one of the bus trips. It was not too satisfactory. I've always wanted to be there on my own, to take my time and see what I wanted to see, to poke into all the corners and to stand and look as long as I wished to stand and look."

"You had a good time, then?"

"Yes, two days of living in the past. And trying to imagine."

She said, "We've lived with it so long, of course, that it's become commonplace with us. We have pride in it, naturally, and a deep interest in it, but it's the tourists who get the most out of it. They come to it fresh and eager and they see it, perhaps, with different eyes than we do."

"That may be right," I said, although I didn't think so.

"But Washington," she said. "There is a place I love. Especially the White House. It fascinates me. I could stand for hours outside that big iron fence and just stare at it."

"You," I said, "and millions of other people. There are always people walking up and down the fence, going slow and looking."

"It's the squirrels I like," she told me. "Those cheeky White House squirrels that come up to the fence and beg and sometimes come right out on the sidewalk and sniff around your feet, then sit up, with their little paws dangling on their chests, looking at you with their beady little eyes."

I laughed, remembering the squirrels. "They're the ones," I said, "who have it made."

"You sound as if you're envious."

"I could be that," I admitted. "The squirrel, I should imagine, has a fairly simple life, while our human life has become so complex that it is never simple. We've made a terrible mess of things. Maybe no worse now than it has ever been, but the point is that it's not getting any better. It's maybe getting worse."

"You're going to put some of that into your book?"

I looked at her in surprise.

"Oh," she said, "everybody knows that you came back to write a book. Did they simply guess or did you tell someone?"

"I suppose that I told George."

"That was enough," she said. "All you have to do is mention anything at all to a single person. Within three hours, flat, everyone in town knows exactly what you said. Before noon tomorrow everyone will know that you walked me home and paid ten dollars for my basket. Whatever possessed you to make a bid like that?"

"It wasn't showing off," I told her. "I suppose some people will think that and I am sorry for it. I suppose I shouldn't have done it, but there were those three louts over against the wall . . ."

She nodded. "I know what you mean. The two Ballard boys and the Williams kid. But you shouldn't mind them. You were fair game to them. New and from a city. They simply had to show you . . ."

"Well, I showed them," I said, "and I suppose it was just as childish of me as it was of them. And with less excuse, for I should know better."

"How long do you plan to stay?" she asked.

I grinned at her. "I'll still be here when you get back in September . . ."

"I didn't mean that."

"I know you didn't. But the book will take awhile. I'm not going to rush it. I'm going to take my time and do the best job of which I'm capable. And I have to catch up with a lot of fishing. Fishing I've been dreaming about all these years. Maybe some hunting in the fall. I imagine this might be a good place for ducks."

"I think it is," she said. "There are a lot of local folks who hunt them every fall and all you hear for weeks is when the northern flight will start coming through."

And that would be the way of it, I knew. That was the lure and the pull of a place like Pilot Knob—the comfortable feeling that you knew what other people were thinking and were able to join with them in a comfortable sort of talk, to sit around the spittle-scarred stove in the store and talk about when the northern flight would be coming through, or about how the fish had started to bite down in Proctor's Slough, or how the last rain had helped the corn or how the violent storm of the night before had put down all the oats and barley. There had been a chair around that stove, I remembered, for my father—a chair held at once by right and privilege. I wondered, as I walked through the lilac-haunted evening, if there'd be a chair for me.

"Here we are," said Kathy, turning into a walk that led up to a large, white, two-story house, all but smothered in trees and shrubbery. I stopped and stared at it, trying to place it, to bring it out of memory.

"The Forsythe place," she said. "The banker Forsythe place. I've boarded here ever since I started teaching here, three years ago."

"But the banker . . ."

"Yes, he's gone. Dead a dozen years or more, I guess. But his widow still lives here. An old, old woman now. Half blind and gets around with a cane. Says she gets lonesome in the big house all alone. That's why she took me in."

"You'll be leaving when?"

"In a day or two. I'm driving back and there is no big hurry. Not a thing to do all summer. Last year I went to summer school, but this year I decided to skip it."

"I may see you again, then, before you leave?" Because for some reason which I didn't try to figure out, I knew that I wanted to see her again.

"Why, I don't know. I'll be busy . . ."

"Tomorrow night, perhaps. Have dinner with me, please. There must be someplace we can drive to. A good dinner and a drink."

"That might be fun," she said.

"I'll call for you," I said. "Will seven be too early?"

"It'll be quite all right," she said, "and thanks for seeing me home."

It was a dismissal, but I hesitated. "Can you get in?" I asked, rather stupidly. "Have you got a key?"

She laughed at me. "I have a key, but there'll be no need to use it. She's waiting for me and watching us right now."

"She?"

"Mrs. Forsythe, of course. Half blind as she is, she knows all that's going on and keeps close watch of me. No harm will ever come to me as long as she's around."

I felt amused and a little angry and upset. I had forgotten, of course—forgotten that you could go nowhere, nor do anything, without someone watching you and knowing and then passing on the information to everyone in Pilot Knob.

"Tomorrow evening," I said a little stiffly, conscious of those eyes watching through the window.

I stood and watched her go up the steps and across the vine-hung porch and before she reached the door, it came open and a flood of light spilled out. Kathy had been right. Mrs. Forsythe had been watching.

I turned about and went through the gate and down the street. The moon had risen over the great bluff to the east of the town, the Pilot Knob which had been a landmark used by pilots in the old steamboating days and which had given the town its name. The moonlight, shining through the massive elm trees which lined the street, made a checkered pattern on the sidewalk and the air was tinged with the smell of lilacs blooming in the yards.

When I came to the schoolhouse corner, I turned down the road that led to the river. Here the village dwindled out and the trees, climbing up the high slope of the bluff, grew thicker, muffling the moonlight.

I had walked only a few feet into this deeper shadow when they jumped me. I'll say this for them—it was a complete surprise. A hurtling body slammed into my legs and bowled me over and when I was going down something else lashed out and struck me in the ribs. I hit the ground and rolled to get out of the way and in the road I heard the sound of feet. I got my knees under me and was halfway up when I saw the shadowy outline of the man in front of me and sensed (not really seeing, just glimpsing a flash of motion) the foot hitting out at me. I twisted to
69

one side and the foot caught me a glancing blow on the arms instead of in the chest, where it apparently had been aimed.

I knew that there were more than one of them, for I had heard the sound of a number of feet out there in the road, and I knew that if I stayed down, they all would rush in, kicking. So I made a great effort to get on my feet and made it, although my stance was shaky. I backed away in an effort to get my feet more squarely under me and I backed into something hard and knew, from the feel of the bark against my back, that I was against a tree.

There were three of them, I saw, poised out in the shadows, darker than the shadows.

The three, I wondered, who had stood against the wall, making fun of me because I was an outsider and fair game. And then lying in wait for me after I'd taken Kathy home.

"All right, you little bastards," I said, "come on in and get it."

They came, all three of them. If I'd had the sense to keep my fool mouth shut, they might not have done it, but at my taunt they did.

I got in just one good lick. I put my fist squarely into the face of the one in the center. The punch I threw was a good one and he was rushing me. The sound of the fist hitting his face was like the sound a sharp axe makes when it hits a frosty tree.

Then fists were hitting me from every side and I felt myself going over and as I fell, they left off with their fists, but they used their feet. I rolled, or tried to roll, up into a ball and protect myself as best I could. It went on for quite a while and I guess I was fairly dizzy, or maybe I passed out for a short while.

The next I remember I was sitting up and the road was empty. I was alone and I was one vast ache, with a few places where the pain had localized a bit. I got to my feet and staggered down the road, reeling a little at first from the dizziness, but finally getting so I could navigate on an even keel.

I reached the motel and got to my room and went into

the bathroom, turning on the light. I was far from a pretty sight. The flesh around one eye was fairly well puffed out and beginning to darken. My face was smeared with blood from half a dozen cuts. Gingerly, I washed off the blood and inspected the cuts and they were not too bad. For several days, of course, I'd have a beauty of an eye.

I think it was my dignity that was hurt worse than the rest of me. Come back to the old home town a minor celebrity from being seen on television and heard on radio and then, one's first evening home, to be beaten up by a gang of rural punks because I had outbid them for the teacher's basket.

Christ, I thought, if this story ever got known in Washington or New York, I'd never hear the last of it.

I felt over my body and I had some bruises here and there, but nothing serious. I'd be sore for a day or two, but that would be the end of it. I'd have to put in a lot of fishing in the next few days, I told myself. Stay out on the river and out of the sight of as many people as I could manage until the swelling around the eye went down. Although, I knew, there was no hope of keeping the story from the good folks of Pilot Knob. And there was my date with Kathy—what would I do about that?

I went to the door and stepped outside to have a last look at the night. The moon now was high over the frowning bluff of Pilot Knob. A slight breeze stirred the trees and set up a furtive rustling of the leaves and suddenly I heard the sound, the far-off cry of many dogs, baying out their hearts.

I caught just a snatch of it, a piece of sound that had been caught and wafted by the wind so that I could hear it, but it now was gone. I stiffened to attention, listening, remembering what Linda Bailey had told me of the were-pack that ran in Lonesome Hollow.

The sound came again, the wild, insistent, heart-chilling clamor of a pack closing in upon its prey. Then the wind shifted once again and the sound was gone.

9

It had been a good day. Not so good for fishing, for I had only four bass on my stringer, but good for being outdoors on the river, good for the chance to renew acquaintance with the river world, for recapturing some of the nuances of a half-forgotten boyhood. Mrs. Streeter had packed a lunch for me and had asked about the black eye and I had been evasive, managing a feeble joke. Then I'd fled to the river and had stayed all day. Not fishing all the time, but exploring as well, poking the canoe into tangled backwaters and little twisting sloughs, looking over an island or two. I told myself that I was smelling out good fishing spots, but I was doing more than that. I was exploring this stretch of water I had dreamed about for years, seeking out the texture of it and the mood, trying to fit myself into this strange world of flowing water, of forested island, of barren and shifting sandbar, and the wooded shores.

Now, with the shadows returning, I headed for the motel, hugging the shore, fighting the current with awkward paddle strokes.

I was a couple of hundred yards from the dock when I heard someone call my name—a whisper that carried across the water.

I lifted my paddle and held it poised, looking at the shore. The current began to carry the canoe slowly down the river.

"In here," the whisper said and I caught a flash of color

at the mouth of a tiny backwater that ran into the shore. I dipped my paddle and drove the canoe into the backwater and there, standing on a log that slanted down the bank with one end anchored in the water, was Kathy Adams. I urged the canoe over until it bumped against the log.

"Jump in," I said. "I'll take you for a cruise."

She stared at me. "That eye!" she said.

I grinned at her. "I ran into a bit of trouble."

"I heard you were in a fight," she said. "I think you are in trouble."

"I'm usually in trouble," I told her, "of one sort or another."

"I mean real trouble this time. They think you killed a man."

"I can easily prove . . ."

"Justin Ballard," she said. "They found his body just an hour or so ago. You fought with him last night."

I nodded. "I think so. It was dark. There were three of them, but I never got a good look at them. The one I hit may have been this Ballard boy. I only hit one of them. After that the other two were all over me."

"It was Justin Ballard you fought with last night," she said. "And the other two. They were bragging around town this morning about it and Justin's face was all smashed up."

"Well, then, that let's me out," I said. "I've been on the river all day long . . ."

And then my words ran out. There was no way to prove I'd been on the river. I'd not seen a soul and probably had been seen by no one.

"I don't understand," I said.

"They were around this morning, bragging about what they'd done to you and they said they were going to hunt you up and finish the job. Then someone found Justin dead and the other two have disappeared."

"They don't think I killed all three?" I asked.

She shook her head. "I don't know what they think about it. The village is shook up. A bunch of them were going to come down here and get you, but George Duncan talked them out of it. He said they shouldn't try to take the law into their own hands. He pointed out there was no proof you'd done it, but the village thinks you did. George called the motel and found you were out fishing. He said for everyone to leave you alone and he called the sheriff. He figured it would be best to let the sheriff handle it."

"But you?" I asked. "You came out to warn me . . ."

"You bought my basket and you walked me home and we made a date," she said. "It sort of seemed to me I should be on your side. I didn't want them to catch you by surprise."

"I'm afraid the date is canceled," I said. "I am very sorry. I had been looking forward to it."

"What are you going to do?"

"I don't know," I said. "I'll have to think about it."

"You haven't got much time."

"I know that. I suppose the only thing is to paddle in and sit and wait for them."

"But they may not wait for the sheriff," she warned.

I shook my head. "There's something in my unit that I have to get. There is something strange about all this."

And there was something strange about it. There had been the rattlesnakes and now, less than twenty hours later, a farm boy dead. Or was it a farm boy dead? Was anybody dead?

"You can't come in now," she told me. "You have to stay out fishing at least until the sheriff gets here. That's why I came to warn you. If there's something in your unit, I can get it for you."

"No," I said.

"There is a back door to all the units," she said, "off the patio that faces on the river. Do you know if that back door is unlocked?"

"I suppose it is," I said.

"I could slip in the back and get . . ."

"Kathy," I said, "I can't . . ."

"You can't come in," she said. "Not for a while, at least."

"You think you could get into the unit?"

75

"I'm sure I could."

"A big manila envelope," I said. "With a Washington postmark and a thick bunch of papers inside. Just get the envelope and then clear out. Keep out of the entire business once you have that envelope."

"This envelope?"

"Nothing incriminating," I said. "Nothing illegal. Just something that must not be seen, information that no one should have."

"It's important?"

"I think it's important, but I can't let you get involved. It wouldn't be . . ."

"I'm already involved," she said. "I've warned you and I suppose that's not very law-abiding, but I couldn't let you just come stumbling into them. You get back on that river and stay there . . ."

"Kathy," I said, "I'm going to tell you something that will shock you. If you're sure you want to take a chance with that envelope."

"I want to do it," she said. "If you tried it, you might be seen. Me, even if I was seen around the place, no one would pay attention."

"All right, then," I said, hating myself for letting her do a dirty job, "I'm not only going out on that river, but I'm going to run, very fast and hard. Not that I've killed anyone, but there's another reason. I suppose the honest thing would be to give myself up, but I find, regretfully, that I have some cowardly tendencies. I can always give myself up, later on, perhaps."

She stared at me, frightened—for which I couldn't blame her. And perhaps with somewhat less regard for me than she'd had to start with.

"If you're going to run," she said, "you'd better start right now."

"One thing," I said.

"Yes?"

"If you get that envelope, don't look inside. Don't read it."

"I don't understand any of this," she said.

"What I don't understand," I told her, "is why you're warning me."

"I've told you that. You might at least say thank you."

"I do, of course," I said.

She began backing up the bank.

"On your way," she said. "I'll get your envelope."

10

Night fell and I did not have to hug the bank so closely, but could get out into the stream, where the current would help me. There had been two towns, but both of them had been on the other side of the river and I had seen their lights, shining across the water and the wide stretch of boggy bottomlands that stretched between the far shore and the river.

I was worried about Kathy. I had no claim to any help from her and I felt considerably like a heel for letting her take on what could turn out to be a very dirty chore. But she had come to warn me, she had aligned herself with me—and she was the only one around. Furthermore, most likely, the only person I could trust. The chances were good, I told myself, that she'd be able to manage it, and it was important, terribly important, it seemed to me, that the manila envelope should be kept from falling into the hands of someone who might make it public.

As soon as possible I'd have to get in touch with Philip and alert him to what was going on. Between the two of us, we might be able to figure out what would be best to do. I had to put some distance between myself and Pilot Knob, then find a telephone—far enough away so that the call would not arouse suspicion.

I was piling up the distance. The current was fast and I helped the speed along as best I could with steady paddle work.

As I drove the canoe along, I was thinking of the night before and about the finding of Justin Ballard's body. And the more I thought about it, the more I became convinced that Ballard had not died. There was no question, it seemed to me, that the three who had attacked me the night before had been the three who had stood ranged against the wall. They had bragged about the beating they had given me and then they had disappeared, but where and how had they disappeared? But wherever or however, with them out of the way, for a time at least, what would be simpler than the planting of a body to enmesh me with the law—perhaps to get me lynched? And if Kathy's version had been true, a lynch party had been forming before George Duncan broke it up. If the things, whatever they were, could fashion out of themselves, or the energy that was themselves, a house, a jacked-up car, a woodpile, two people, a supper on the table, a jug of good corn whiskey, they could do anything. A dead and rigid body would be a cinch for them. And also, I realized, they could bring their abilities to bear upon keeping the missing three from showing up until it made no difference. It was a crazy way to do things, certainly, accomplishment by indirection, but no crazier than killing a man with a car that disappeared, or the strange and elaborate scheme which they'd gone about to introduce a potential victim to a den of rattlesnakes.

Soon, I hoped, there'd be a river town where I could find a public telephone booth and put in my call. The alarm might have spread by now and the river towns might be watched, although there would be no certainty in the sheriff's mind that I had fled downriver. No certainty, of course, unless Kathy had been apprehended. I tried to turn off this thought, but try as I might it kept coming back to me. But even watched, I probably could make it. And after I had made my call, what did I do then? Surrender myself, perhaps, although that was something that had to be decided later. I could, I realized, have surrendered myself and still made the call to Philip, but it would have been made within the hearing of an officer and there'd have been no opportunity to do anything after it was made.

I wasn't entirely satisfied with the way I'd handled the situation and I felt a sense of guilt, but as I beat it back and forth in my mind I could see no other acceptable alternative.

Night had fallen, but a faint light still hung above the river. From the shore came the distant lowing of a cow and the faint barking of a dog. All about me the water whispered with its eternal talk and at times a fish flopped, making a sudden plop and setting up a concentric eddy of ripples. I seemed to be moving across a great plain; the dark, tree-lined river banks and the distant hills were simply shadows at the periphery of the plain. It was a deeply peaceful place, this realm of water and of shadow. Strangely, I felt safe out there on the river. Detached might be a better word. I was alone and in the center of a tiny universe and the universe stretched out on every side, untenanted. The sounds that came across the water, the lowing of the cow and the barking of the dog, had so much the sense of distance in them that they accentuated, rather than destroyed, the smug sense of detachment.

Then the detachment ended. In front of me the water humped and as I paddled frantically to steer free of the hump, a blackness rose up out of the river—yards and yards of blackness, with water streaming off it.

The chain of blackness reared into the air, a great, long, sinuous neck with a nightmare head attached. It came up into the air and bent in a graceful curve so that the head hung just above me, and looking up, I stared in fascinated fear into the red, jewellike eyes that glittered in the faint light reflected from the surface of the water. A forked tongue flickered out at me and then the mouth came open and I saw the fangs.

I dipped the paddle and with a mighty heave drove the canoe forward in a sudden surge. I felt the hot breath of the beast upon my neck as the lunging head missed me by bare inches.

Glancing back over my shoulder, I saw the head poised again, ready for another strike and I knew that the odds were stacked heavily against me. I'd fooled the creature once; I doubted that I'd be able to do it a second time. The shore was too far away to reach and the only thing that was left for me to do was to dodge and run. For a moment the thought of abandoning the canoe crossed my mind, but I was not too good a swimmer and this was some sort of water monster that undoubtedly could scoop me out of the water with remarkable ease.

It was taking its time now. It didn't need to hurry. It knew it had me, but this time it wasn't going to take a chance of missing. Water rippled behind it in a neat V as it moved toward me, the long neck curved and ready, the head with jaws agape, the fangs shining in the starlight.

I swung the canoe sharply in the hope of catching it off balance, forcing it to get squared around again to make a new approach.

As I swung the canoe sharply some object rolled and rattled in its bottom. And when I heard that rattle, I knew what I had to do—no reason to it, no logic, it was just plain damn silly, but I was at the end of my rope and fast running out of time. I had no hope that I could do what I planned to do—well, not a plan, more like a reflex response—and no idea what I'd do if it really worked. But I had to do it. Mostly, I suppose, because it was the only thing that I could think of doing.

I hit the water a lick with the paddle to turn the canoe end for end, so I could face the creature. Then I reached down and picked up the rod and stood up. A canoe ordinarily is not the sort of craft a man should stand up in, but this one was fairly steady and I'd been doing some practicing, standing up in it, that afternoon.

I had a bass plug hooked onto the line and it was a fairly heavy plug (perhaps a bit too heavy for good bass fishing) and it had three gang hooks in it.

The critter was fairly close now and its mouth still was open wide, so I brought the rod back and I aimed, in my mind, where I wanted that plug to go and I swung my arm.

I watched in fascination as the plug flashed out, the metal of it glittering just a bit in the river light. And it plopped into that open mouth and I waited for a split second, then lifted the rod tip and lunged back hard with all my strength to set the hooks. I felt the tug as the hooks bit deep and there I was, with the monster hooked.

I hadn't thought beyond the casting of the plug. I hadn't figured out what I would do if I hooked the monster. Mostly, I suppose, because I had not thought for an instant that I would really hook him.

But now, having hooked him, I did the only thing I could. I dropped quickly into a crouch and held fast to the rod. The monster's head jerked back and pointed sharply toward the sky and the reel was singing as the line went out.

I jerked the rod again to set the hooks still deeper and out in the water in front of me a tidal wave went into action. A mighty body heaved into the air and it kept on coming and I thought it would never stop. The head, on its lanky neck, was thrashing back and forth and the rod was whipping wildly and I hung onto it like grim death, although I can't imagine why I hung onto it. One thing for certain, I didn't want this fish that I had hooked.

The canoe was pitching and bucking in the waves set up by the creature's struggles and I crouched lower in it, huddling in it, with my elbows braced against the gunwales, trying to keep the center of gravity low to prevent an upset. And now the canoe began to move, faster and faster, down the river, towed behind the fleeing creature.

And through it all, I hung onto the rod. I could have let go of it, I could have thrown it away, but I hung onto it and as the canoe started to move I whooped in jeering triumph. The thing had been chasing me and I had been the hunted, but now I had it hooked and it was running in pain and panic and so far as I was concerned I was set to run it ragged.

The thing went streaking down the river and the line was thrumming and the canoe was riding high and fast and I whooped like a zany cowboy astride a bucking horse. I forgot for a moment what was going on or what had led up to it. It was a wild ride through the night of this river world and ahead of me the creature was twisting and humping, with the serrated row of fins along its back sometimes arched into the air and sometimes low against the water and awash in the turmoil of its struggle.

Suddenly the line went slack and the creature disappeared. I was alone upon the river, crouching in a canoe that was bucking up and down in the turbulence of the water. As the water quieted, I eased myself back upon the seat and began reeling in the line. There was a lot of reeling to be done, but finally the plug came clattering aboard and snugged against the rod tip. I was somewhat astonished to see the plug, for I had thought the line had snapped and that with the snapping of it, the creature had sounded and made its escape. But now it became apparent that the creature had simply disappeared, for the hooks must have been set deeply and solidly into its flesh and the only way that the plug could have come clean was for the flesh in which it had been embedded to have disappeared.

The canoe now was floating gently on the river and I reached down and picked up the paddle. The moon was rising and the sky glow of its rising made the river glisten like a road of flowing silver. I sat quietly with the paddle in my hand and wondered what to do. The instinctive thing was to get off the river before another monster came heaving from the depths, to get busy with the paddle and head in for shore. But I felt sure, on second thought, that there'd not be another monster—for the business of the monster could only be explained if it were considered in the same frame of reference as the den of rattlesnakes and Justin Ballard's death. My old friend's other world had tried another gambit and had failed again, and it was not in the nature of their operation, I was sure, to repeat a scheme that failed. And if that reasoning was valid, for the moment at least the river probably was the safest place in all the world for me to be.

A sharp, shrill piping broke my line of thought and I swung my head around to try to identify the origin of the piping. Squatted on the gunwale, eight feet or so away, perched a little monstrosity. It was grotesquely humanoid and covered by a heavy coat of hair and it clung to its perch with a pair of feet that resembled the talons of an owl. Its head rose to a point and the hair grew from the top of this point to fall about the head in such a manner as to provide a hat resembling those worn by natives in certain Asian countries. Projecting from the side of its head were juglike, pointed ears and its eyes glared redly at me from behind the hanging mat of hair.

Now that I saw it, its piping began to make some sense. "Three times is a charm!" it was saying, gleefully, in its high, shrill piping. "Three times is a charm! Three times is a charm!"

Gorge rising in my throat, I swung the paddle hard. The flat side of the blade caught the little monstrosity sharply and popped it off the gunwale, high into the air, as a high fly might be hit by a baseball bat. The piping changed into a feeble scream and I watched it in some fascination as it sailed high above the river, finally reaching the top of its parabola and starting to come down. Halfway down it blinked out, like the bursting of a soap bubble—one moment there, the next moment gone.

I got down to work with the paddle. I was looking for a town and there was no use fooling myself any longer. The quicker I reached a phone and put in a call to Philip, the better it would be.

My old friend might not have been entirely right in all that he had written, but there was something damn funny going on.

11

The town was small and I could find no phone booth. Nor was I absolutely sure what town it was, although, if my memory did not play me false, it was a place called Woodman. I tried to summon up in my head a map of the locality, but the town and the country were too far in the past and I could not be sure of it. But the name of the town, I told myself, was not important; the important thing was to place that phone call. Philip was in Washington and he'd know what was best to do—and even if he didn't know what to do, he at least should know what was going on. I owed him that much for sending me the copy of his uncle's notes. Although I knew that if he had not sent them to me, I might not be in this mess.

The only place in the block-long business district that still was open was a bar. Yellow light shone dimly through its dirt-grimed windows and a slight breeze blowing up the street set a beer sign to creaking back and forth upon its iron bracket suspended above the sidewalk.

I stood across the street, trying to screw up my courage to go in the bar. There was no guarantee, of course, that the place would have a phone, although it seemed likely that it would. I knew that in stepping across the threshold of the place I'd be running a certain amount of risk, for it was almost certain that by now the sheriff would have put out an alarm concerning me. The alarm might not have reached this place, of course, but it still was a chance to take.

The canoe was down at the river landing, tied to a tottery post, and all I had to do was to go back and get into it and push out into the stream. No one would be the wiser, for no one had seen me. Except for the place across the street, the town was positively dead.

But I had to make that phone call; I simply had to make it. Philip should be warned, and I might already be too late. Once warned, he might have some suggestion of something we could do. It was apparent now that anyone who read what my old dead friend had written faced the same danger that he had faced in writing it.

I stood in an agony of indecision and finally, scarcely realizing I was doing it, I started walking across the street. When I reached the sidewalk, I stopped and looked up at the creaking sign and the creaking seemed to wake me up to what I had been about to do. I was a hunted man and there was no sense in walking in there and asking for the kind of trouble that I was apt to get. I walked on past the bar, but halfway down the street I turned about and started back again and when I did that, I knew it was no use. I could go on like that, walking back and forth all night, not knowing what to do.

So I climbed the steps and pushed open the door. A man was hunched over the bar at the far end of the room and a bartender was leaning on the bar, facing the door, looking as if he'd been waiting there all night for customers to come in. The rest of the place was empty, with the chairs pushed in close against the tables.

The bartender didn't move. It was as if he didn't see me. I stepped in and closed the door, then walked over to the bar.

"What'll it be, mister?" the bartender asked me.

"Bourbon," I said. I didn't ask for ice; it looked like the sort of place where it might be a breach of etiquette to ask for a piece of ice. "And some change—that is, if you have a phone."

The man jerked his thumb toward a corner of the room. "Over there," he said. I looked and the booth was there, jammed into the corner.

"That's quite an eye you have," he said.

"Yes, isn't it," I told him.

He set a glass out on the bar and poured.

"Traveling late," he said.

"Sort of," I told him. Glancing at my wristwatch, I saw that it was eleven thirty.

"Didn't hear no car."

"Left it up the street a ways. I thought the town was all shut up. Then I saw your light."

It wasn't much of a story, but he didn't question it. He didn't care. He was just making conversation.

"I'm about ready to close up," he said. "Have to close at midnight. But there's no one here tonight. Except old Joe over there. He is always here. Every night, at closing time, I put him out. Just like a goddamn cat."

The liquor wasn't too good, but I needed it. It put some warmth inside of me and helped to cut the phlegm of fear that was clogging up my throat.

I handed him a bill.

"Want all of this in change?"

"If you can manage it."

"I can manage it, all right. You must be figuring on making quite a call."

"Washington," I said. I saw no reason not to tell him.

He gave me the change and I walked to the phone booth with it and put in the call. I didn't know Phil's number and it took a little while. Then I heard the ringing and a moment later someone was answering.

"Mr. Philip Freeman, please," the operator said. "Long distance calling."

A gasp came from the other end of the line, then a silence. Finally, the voice said, "He's not here."

"Do you know when he'll be in?" asked the operator.

"He won't be in," said the strangled voice. "I don't know, operator. Is this some sort of joke? Philip Freeman's dead."

"Your party can't come to the phone," the operator told me in her computer voice. "I am informed . . ."

"Never mind," I said. "I'll talk to whoever's on the line."

"Please deposit a dollar and a half," said the computer voice.

I reached into my pocket and brought out a handful of

change, fumbling with it, dropping some of it on the floor. My hand was trembling so badly that it was difficult to feed the coins into the slots.

Philip Freeman dead!

I managed to get the last coin in. "Go ahead," said the operator.

"Are you still there?" I asked.

"Yes," said the ghostly, shaken voice at the other end.

"I am sorry," I said. "I didn't know. I am Horton Smith, an old friend of Philip's."

"I've heard him speak of you. I am Philip's sister."

"Marge?" I asked.

"Yes, Marge."

"When did . . ."

"This evening," she said. "Phyllis was supposed to pick him up. He was standing on the sidewalk waiting for her, and then he just fell over."

"Heart attack?"

There was a long silence and then she said, "That is what we think. That's what Phyllis thinks, but . . ."

"How is Phyllis?"

"She is sleeping now. The doctor gave her something."

"I can't tell you how sorry I am," I told her. "You said this evening?"

"Just a few hours ago. And, Mr. Smith, I don't know—I don't think maybe I should say this. But you were Philip's friend . . ."

"For many years," I said.

"There is something strange. Some of the people who saw him fall said he was shot by an arrow—an arrow through the heart. But there was no arrow. Some witnesses told the police and now the coroner . . ."

Her voice broke and the sound of weeping came along the wire. Then she said, "You knew Philip and you knew Uncle, too."

"Yes, the two of them."

"It doesn't seem possible. The two of them so close together."

"It seems impossible," I said.

"Was there something? You asked for Philip . . ."

"Nothing now," I said. "I'm coming back to Washington."

"I think the funeral will be Friday."

"Thank you. I'm sorry for breaking in like this."

"You couldn't know," she said. "I'll tell Phyllis that you called."

"If you would," I told her. Although, actually, it made little difference. She'd not remember me. I'd met Philip's wife only once or twice.

We said good night and I sat dazed in the booth. Philip dead—shot down by an arrow. Arrows were not used today to get rid of people. Nor were, for that matter, such things as sea serpents or a den of rattlesnakes.

I stooped down and fumbled around, picking up the money I had dropped.

Something was tapping at the door of the booth and I looked up. The bartender had his face pressed against the window and when he saw me look up, he quit his tapping and waved his hand at me. I straightened and opened the door.

"What's the matter with you?" he asked. "You sick or something?"

"No. I just dropped some change."

"If you want another drink, you just got time for it. I am closing up."

"I have to make another call," I said.

"Make it snappy, then," he told me.

I found a telephone directory on a shelf underneath the phone.

"Where do I look for a Pilot Knob number?" I asked.

"You'll find it in there. Section called Pilot Knob-Woodman."

"This is Woodman?"

"Sure it is," said the man, disgusted with me. "You must have missed the signboard just outside of town."

"I guess I did," I said.

I closed the door and found the section, then thumbed through the pages to find the name I wanted. Finally I located it—Mrs. Janet Forsythe. There was only the one Forsythe in the book. Otherwise I'd not have known who to call. I had never known or had forgotten the name of Old Doc Forsythe's wife.

I reached out to lift the hook off the receiver, then hesitated. I had gotten by so far. Had I ought to take another chance? But there was no way, I argued, in which the call could be detected.

I lifted the receiver, fed in the coin, and dialed. I waited while the ringing went on and on. Finally the ringing broke off and someone said hello. I thought I recognized the voice, but I couldn't be sure.

"Miss Adams?" I asked.

"This is she. Mrs. Forsythe is asleep and . . ."

"Kathy," I said.

"Who is this?"

"Horton Smith," I said.

"Oh," she said, startled. Then said nothing more.

"Kathy . . ."

"I am glad you called," she said. "It was all a big mistake. The Ballard boy turned up. All three of them turned up. Now it is all right and . . ."

"Hold up a minute, please," I said. She was talking so fast that the words were tripping over one another. "If the Ballard kid turned up, tell me what happened to the body."

"The body? Oh, you mean . . ."

"Yes, the body of Justin Ballard."

"Horton, that's the strangest thing of all. The body disappeared."

"What do you mean—disappeared?" I thought I knew. I just wanted to be sure.

"Why, they found it out at the edge of the woods just west of town and they left two men—Tom Williams was one of them, I don't know who the other was—to watch it until the sheriff came. The two men looked away for a minute and when they looked back the body wasn't there. No one could have stolen it. It just disappeared. The whole town is in an uproar . . ."

"And you?" I asked. "Did you get the envelope?"

"Yes, I got it. And I had just gotten home when the body disappeared."

"So now everything's all right?"

"Yes, of course," she said. "You can come back now."

"Tell me one thing, Kathy. Did you look at what was in that envelope?"

She started to speak and hesitated.

"Look, Kathy, this is important. Did you look at it?"

"I just took a peek and . . ."

"Damn it," I shouted, "quit stalling! Tell me if you read it."

She flared at me. "All right, I read it. I think the man who wrote it . . ."

"Never mind about the man who wrote it. How much did you read? All of it?"

"The first few pages. To where the notes began. Horton, do you mean to tell me there is something to it? But that's a silly thing to ask. Of course there couldn't be. I don't know a thing about evolution, but I could punch a lot of holes in it."

"Don't waste your time punching holes," I told her. "Whatever made you read it?"

"Well, I guess because you told me not to. When you told me that, I couldn't help but read it. It's your fault that I read it. And what's wrong with reading it?"

What she said was true, of course, although I hadn't thought of it at the time. I had warned her because I didn't want her to get further involved and I had done the one thing that had been guaranteed to get her involved, clear up to her neck. And the worst thing about Kathy was that she need not have been involved, that there had been no reason for her to get that envelope. The body of Justin Ballard had disappared and with the disappearance I no longer was suspect. But if it had not happened that way, I told myself, trying to justify the circumstance, the sheriff would have searched my room at the motel and have found the envelope and then there'd have been hell to pay.

"There's only one thing wrong with it," I told her. "You're in trouble now. You . . ."

"Horton Smith," she snapped, "don't you threaten me!"

"I'm not threatening you," I said. "I'm just sorry. I never should have let you . . ."

"Sorry about what?" she asked.

"Kathy," I pleaded, "listen to me and don't argue. How soon can you get away? You planned to drive back to Pennsylvania. Are you ready now?"

"Why, yes," she said. "My bags are packed—but what does that have to do with this?"

"Kathy . . ." I began, then stopped. It would frighten her and I didn't want that. But I could think of no easy way to tell her.

"Kathy," I said, "the man who wrote what is in the envelope was killed; the man who sent it to me was killed just a few hours ago . . ."

She gasped. "And you think that I . . ."

"Don't be a fool," I said. "Anyone who reads what's in that envelope is in danger."

"And you? Was the business of Justin . . ."

"I think it was," I said.

"What should I do?" she asked. Not particularly frightened, perfectly matter-of-fact, perhaps somewhat unbelieving.

"You can get into your car and come and pick me up. Bring along the envelope, so no one else can get it."

"Pick you up. Then what?"

"Then head for Washington. There are people there to see."

"Like who?"

"Like the FBI, for one," I said.

"But you can simply pick up a phone . . ."

"Not on this one," I shouted. "Not on something like this. To start with, they'd not believe a phone call. They get a lot of crank calls."

"But you think you can convince them."

"Maybe not," I said. "Apparently you are not convinced."

"I don't know if I am or not. I'd have to think about it."

"There's no time to think," I warned her. "You either come and pick me up, or you don't. It might be safer if we traveled together, although I can't guarantee it would be. You're traveling east in any case and . . ."

"Where are you now?" she asked.

"Woodman. A town down the river."

"I know where it is. Do you want me to pick up some of your stuff at the motel?"

"No," I said. "I think time may be important. We can take turns driving. Only stop for gas and food."

"Where will I find you?"

"Just drive slowly down the main street. It's the only street there is—the state highway. I'll be watching for you. There won't be many cars through here tonight, I would imagine."

"I feel foolish," she said. "This is so . . ."

"Melodramatic," I suggested.

"I suppose you could call it that. But, as you say, I am driving east in any case."

"I'll be watching for you."

"I'll be there," she said, "in half an hour. Maybe a little more."

Out of the phone booth, I found that the muscles of my legs were cramped from being hunched in the crowded space. I limped across to the bar.

"You took your time," the bartender said, sourly. "I already threw Joe out and it's closing time. Here's your drink. Don't linger over it."

I picked up the glass. "I'd be honored if you'd join me."

"You mean have a drink with you?"

I nodded.

He shook his head. "I don't drink," he said.

I finished off the drink and paid him and walked out. Behind me, the lights went out and a moment later the bartender came out and locked the door. He tripped over something as he stepped out on the sidewalk, but righted himself and reached down and picked up what he had stumbled over. It was a baseball bat.

"Damn kids were playing out in back after suppertime," he said. "One of them left it here."

Disgusted, he pitched it onto a bench that stood beside the door.

"I don't see your car," he said.

"I haven't got a car."

"But you said . . ."

"I know. But if I'd told you I didn't have a car it would have required a lot of explanation and I had to get those phone calls made."

He looked at me, shaking his head—a man who popped out of nowhere and didn't have a car.

"I came by canoe," I said. "I tied up at the landing."

"And what are you going to do now?"

"Stay right here," I said. "I'm waiting for a friend."

"The one you called?"

"Yes," I said. "The one I called."

"Well, good night," he said. "I hope you don't have to wait too long."

He went down the street, heading home, but several times he slowed and half turned, to look back at me.

12

Somewhere in the wood along the river an owl muttered querulously. The night wind held a biting edge and I turned up the collar of my shirt to gain a little warmth against it. A prowling cat came pussyfooting down the street, stopped when it caught sight of me, and then angled over to the opposite side of the street to disappear in the darkness between two buildings.

With the disappearance of the bartender, Woodman took on the feel of a deserted village. I had not paid much attention to it before, but now, with time to be used up, I saw that the place was tattered and down-at-heels, another one of those dying little towns, somewhat further along the road to oblivion than was Pilot Knob. The sidewalks were breaking up and in places grass and weeds grew in the cracks. The buildings bore the marks of time, unpainted and unrepaired, and the architecture, if the shape of them could be dignified by such a word, dated to a century before. There had been a time—there must have been a time—when the town had been brand-new and hopeful; there must then have been some economic reason for its planting and existence. And the reason, I knew, must have been the river, at a time when the river still served as an artery of commerce, when the produce of the farm or mill was brought to the river landing to be loaded on the steamboats, when the same steamboats freighted all the goods that were needed by the countryside. But the river had long since lost its economic role and had been turned back to the wildness of its strip of bottomland. The railroad and the high-speed highways, the planes flying far above it, had robbed it of all significance except the primal, basic significance it had always held in the land's ecology.

And now Woodman stood forlorn, as truly a backwater in the fabric of society as the many little backwaters which meandered out from the mainstream of the river. Once prosperous, perhaps, but now in poverty, it hung on doggedly as a small dot upon the map (although not on every map), as a living place for people who had as much lost touch with the world as had the town itself. The world had gone marching on, but little, dying towns such as this had not done any marching; they had dozed and fallen out of step and perhaps they no longer cared much about the world or the other people in it. They had retained, or created, or clung to a world that belonged to them, or that they belonged to. And thinking about it, I realized that the definition of what had happened here did not really matter, for the town itself no longer really mattered. It was a pity, I thought, that this should be, for in these little dozing, forgotten and forgetting towns there still existed a rare touch of human caring and compassion, of human value, that the world had need of and could use, but which it had largely lost.

Here, in towns such as this, people still heard the imagined baying of the were-pack, while the rest of the world listened for an uglier sound that might precede the thunderclap of atomic doom. Between the two of them, it seemed to be, the were-pack might be the saner sound to hear. For if the provincialism of little towns like this was madness, it was a very gentle, even a pleasant, madness, while the madness of the outer world was stripped of any gentleness.

Kathy would be arriving soon—or I hoped she would arrive. If she failed to show up, it would be understandable. She had said she would, but on second thought, I warned myself, she might decide against it. I, myself, I recalled, had questioned very seriously what my old friend had written, although I had more reason at the time to believe it than Kathy would have now.

And if she did not show up, what should I do then? Go

back to Pilot Knob, most likely, gather up my things and head for Washington. Although I was not entirely sure how much good going there would do. The FBI, I wondered, or the CIA? Or who? Someone who would listen, someone who would pay attention and not brush it off as the raving of a madman.

I was leaning against the side of the building which housed the bar, looking up the street, hoping that Kathy would show up very soon, when I saw the wolf come trotting down the road.

There is something about a wolf, some deep-buried instinct from man's distant past, that triggers at once a chill of fright and a raising of the hackles. Here, immediately, is an implacable enemy, a killer as terrible and remorseless as is man himself. There is nothing noble about this killer. He is sly and tricky and ruthless and relentless. There can be no compromise between him and man, for the enmity is one of too long standing.

Standing there, seeing the wolf trot out of the darkness, I felt this instant chill, this raising of the hackles.

The wolf moved self-assuredly. About him there was no slinking and no furtiveness. He was going about his business and would brook no foolishness. He was big and black, or at least he looked black in the night, but gaunt and he had a hungry look about him.

I stepped out from the building and as I stepped out, I cast a quick look about me for something that might serve as a weapon, and there, lying on the bench where the bartender had tossed it, was the baseball bat. I reached down and took hold of the bat and lifted it. It had a nice heft and a good balance to it.

When I looked back at the street, there was not one wolf, but three, spread out one behind the other, all three of them trotting with that irritating self-assurance.

I stood still on the sidewalk, with the bat gripped in my hand, and when the first wolf reached a point opposite me it stopped and wheeled around to face me.

I suppose I could have shouted and aroused the town; I could have called for help. But the thought of shouting never once occurred to me. This was a matter between myself and these three wolves—no, not three, for there were more of them now, trotting out of the darkness and coming down the street.

I knew they weren't wolves, not real wolves, not honest wolves born and raised on this honest earth. No more real wolves than the sea serpent had been a real sea serpent. These were the things I knew, that Linda Bailey had told me about; perhaps the very ones that I had heard the night before when I had stepped out for a breath of air. Linda Bailey had said dogs, but they weren't dogs. They were an ancient fear that stretched clear back to the primal days of mankind, a fear that had bayed its way through uncounted centuries, made whole and sound and material by those very centuries of fear.

As if, for all the world, they were performing a well-rehearsed drill maneuver, the wolves came trotting in, aligning themselves with the first of them, swinging around to face me. When they all were there, they sat down as if someone had barked an order, sitting in a row, in identical position, sitting straight, but easy, with their front legs well under them and very neatly placed. They sat there facing me and they let their tongues hang out the sides of their mouths as they panted most demurely. They all were looking at me and looking nowhere else.

I counted them and there were an even dozen.

I shifted the bat to get a better grip upon it, but I knew there wasn't much hope if they tried to rush me. If they rushed me, I knew, they'd do it all together, as they'd done everything else together. A baseball bat, well swung, is a deadly weapon and I knew I'd get a few of them, but I couldn't get them all. I could, just possibly, make a leap for the metal bracket from which the beer sign hung, but I had grave doubt that it would hold my weight. It already was canted at a sagging angle and quite possibly the screws, or bolts, that held it would rip from the rotten wood at the slightest strain.

There was only one thing to do, I told myself—stand fast and face it out.

I had taken my eyes off the wolves for an instant to

glance up at the sign and when I looked back again the little monstrosity with the pointed head was standing in front of the wolves.

"I should let them have you," he piped, ferociously. "Out there on the river you hadn't ought to belted me with that paddle."

"If you don't shut your trap," I told him, "I'll belt you with this ball bat."

He bounced up and down in rage. "Such ingratitude!" he screeched. "If it weren't for the rules . . ."

"What rules?" I asked.

"You should know," he piped in wrath. "It is you humans who have made them."

And then it struck me. "You mean that business about three times is a charm?"

"Unfortunately," he shrilled, "that is what I mean."

"After you jokers have failed three times in a row, I am off the hook?"

"That is it," he said.

I looked at the wolves. They were sitting there, with their tongues hanging out, grinning at me. They didn't care, I sensed. It was all one to them if they took me or if they went trotting off.

"But there is further," said the thing with the pointed head.

"You mean there is a catch to it."

"Oh, not at all," it said. "There is the matter of honest chivalry."

I wondered what chivalry might have to do with it, but I didn't ask. I knew that he would tell me. He wanted me to ask; he was still stinging from that paddle blow and he was all set to do a good job baiting me.

He glared at me from beneath the hanging fringe of hair and waited. I took a good grip on the ball bat and waited in my turn. The wolves were enjoying it immensely. They sat in silent laughter.

Finally he could stand it no longer.

"You have," he said, "your three-times charm. But there is another one who hasn't."

He had me cold and he knew he had me cold and it was a lucky thing for him that he was beyond the ball bat's reach.

"You mean Miss Adams," I said, as coolly as I could.

"You catch on, quick," he said. "Will you, as a chivalrous gentleman, take her peril upon your shoulders? Had it not been for you, she'd not be vulnerable. I think you owe it to her."

"So do I," I said.

"You mean that?" the critter cried in glee.

"Indeed I do," I told him.

"You take upon your shoulders . . ."

I interrupted him. "Cut out the oratory. I have said I would."

Maybe I could have stretched it out, but if I did I sensed I would lose face and had a hunch that face might count for something in the situation.

The wolves came to their feet and they quit their panting and there was now no laughter in them.

My mind spun in a frantic whirl to snare some course of action that might give me a chance to fight my way out of this dilemma. But it was empty whirling. I got not the least idea.

The wolves paced slowly forward, purposeful and businesslike. They had a job to do and they intended doing it and getting it over with. I backed away. With my back against the building, I might have a better chance. I swished the bat at them and they halted momentarily, then came on again. My back against the building, I stopped and waited for them.

A fan of light caught the building opposite and swiveled swiftly to point down the street toward us. Two blinding headlights loomed out of the darkness. An engine howled its protest at swift acceleration and through the howl came the scream of tortured tires.

The wolves whirled, crouching, held for an instant, pinpointed on the beam of light, then moved, but some of them too slowly as the car came plowing into them. There was the sickening sound of impact as metal crunched into flesh and bone. Then the wolves were gone, blinking out

102

as the thing with the pointed head had blinked out above the water when I'd smacked it with the paddle.

The car was slowing and I ran after it, as fast as I could go. Not that there was any danger now, but I knew that I'd feel safer once I got inside that car.

It came to a halt and I made it to the door and climbed into the seat and slammed the door and locked it.

"One down and two to go," I said.

Kathy's voice was shaky. "One down?" she asked. "What do you mean by that?" She was trying to be casual, but not succeeding very well.

I reached out in the darkness and touched her and I could feel that she was trembling. God knows, she had the right to.

I pulled her close and held her and she clung to me and all around us the darkness was vibrating with an ancient fear and mystery.

"What were those things?" she asked in a quavery voice. "They had you backed up against the wall and they looked like wolves."

"They were, indeed," I said. "Very special wolves."

"Special?"

"Werewolves. At least I think they were."

"But, Horton . . ."

"You read the paper," I said. "When you shouldn't have. You should know by now . . ."

She pulled away from me. "But that can't be true," she said in a tight, schoolteacherish tone. "There just can't be werewolves and goblins and all the rest of it."

I laughed softly—not that I was enjoying myself, but amused by the fierceness of her protest.

"There weren't," I told her, "until a flighty little primate came along and dreamed them up."

She sat for a moment, staring at me. "But they were there," she said.

I nodded. "They would have had me if you hadn't come along."

"I drove too fast," she said. "Too fast all the way for the sort of road it was. I scolded myself for doing it, but it seemed I had to. Now I'm glad I did."

103

"So am I," I said.

"What do we do now?"

"We drive on. Without wasting time. Without stopping for a minute."

"Gettysburg, you mean."

"That's where you want to go."

"Yes, of course. But you said Washington."

"I have to get to Washington. As fast as I can get there. Perhaps it would be better . . ."

"If I went with you, right on to Washington."

"If you would. It might be a whole lot safer."

And wondered what I was talking about. How could I guarantee her safety?

"Maybe we had better start then. It's a long way to go. Would you drive, Horton, please?"

"Certainly," I said and opened the door.

"No, don't," she said. "Don't get out."

"I have to walk around."

"We could change seats. Slide past one another."

I laughed at her. I'd gotten terribly brave. "I am safe," I said, "with this baseball bat. Besides, there's nothing out there now."

But I was wrong. There was something out there now. It was clambering up the side of the car and as I stepped out it hoisted itself atop the hood. It turned around and faced me, jigging in its rage. Its pointed head was quivering and its pointed ears were flapping and the thatch of hanging hair bounced up and down.

"I am the Referee," it shrilled at me. "You fight very tricky. For such dirty fighting back, there must be penalty. I call a foul upon you!"

I swung the bat in rage, two-handed. For one night I'd had enough of this strange character.

It didn't wait. It knew what to expect. It flickered and went away and the bat went swishing through the empty air.

13

I slumped in the seat and tried to sleep, but I couldn't seem to sleep. My body needed sleep, but my brain cried out against it. I sank close to the edge of it, but never seemed quite able to drop off into it.

A parade went marching through my brain and there was no end to it and no reason, either. It was not really thinking, for I was too played out to think. I had been at the wheel too long; all night until an early morning stop for breakfast somewhere near Chicago and then driving against the rising sun until Kathy took the wheel. I had tried to sleep then and had napped a little, but I hadn't gotten much rest. And now, after lunch somewhere near the Pennsylvania line, I had settled down, determined to build up some sack time. But it wasn't working out.

The wolves came again, padding down my brain in the same nonchalant manner as they had padded down the street of Woodman. They closed in upon me as I backed against the building and, although I was watching for her and waiting for her, Kathy did not come. They closed in upon me and I fought them off, realizing that in the end I could not fight them off, while the Referee perched upon the bracket that held the creaking sign and in his piping voice was yelling foul at me. My legs and arms grew heavy and I had trouble moving them, my body aching and sweating in a desperate effort to make them move the way they should. The blows I struck with the bat seemed to be feeble blows, although I put all the strength I had into the striking of the blows and I wondered and worried most intensely why this should be so until the realization dawned upon me slowly that I held no baseball bat, but a writhing, limber rattlesnake.

At the realization, the snake and the wolves and Woodman faded from my mind and I was talking once again with my old friend huddled in the chair that threatened to engulf him. He gestured toward the doors that opened on the patio and, following his gesture, I saw that the sky was tenanted by a fairy landscape with ancient, twisted oaks and a castle that thrust snow-white spires and turrets far into the air, while on the road that went winding up the wild and breathless crags leading to the castle marched a motley throng of assorted knights and monsters. I think that we are haunted, my old friend told me, and he had no more than said these words when an arrow came whizzing past my head and sank deep into his chest. Off in the wings, as if this place where I stood was some sort of stage, a sweet voice began declaiming: Who shot Cock Robin? I said the Sparrow . . . and looking very closely I could see with clarity that my old friend, with an arrow in his chest, was certainly no robin, but surely was a sparrow and I wondered if he'd been shot by another sparrow or if I had misunderstood and it had been a robin that had shot a sparrow. And I said to the little monstrosity with the pointed head, which was the Referee, now perching on the mantle, why don't you yell foul, for it is, indeed, a most foul thing that a friend is done to death. Although I couldn't be sure if he were done to death or not, for he still sat as he had before, engulfed in the chair, with a smile upon his lips and there was no blood where the arrow had gone in.

Then, like the wolves in Woodman, my old friend and his study went away and for an instant the slate of my mind was clean and I rejoiced at it, but almost immediately I was running down an avenue and ahead of me I saw a building that I recognized and I strived mightily to reach it, for it was important that I reach it and finally I did. Sitting at a desk just inside the door was an agent of the FBI. I knew he was an agent because he had square shoulders and an angular jaw and wore a soft black hat. I leaned my mouth close to his ear and whispered about a terrible secret that must be told to no one, for it was death to anyone who knew it. He listened to me with no change of expression, without a single twitch of a muscle in his face and when I had finished, he reached for a phone. You are a member of the Mob, he told me, I can recognize one of them at a hundred paces. And then I saw that I had been mistaken, that he was no agent of the FBI, but merely Superman. His place immediately was taken by another man in another place—a tall man standing dignified and rigid, with white hair combed meticulously and a clipped, white, bristly mustache. I knew him immediately for what he was, an agent of the CIA, and I stood tall, on tiptoes, to whisper in his ear, being very careful to tell him, in its exact phraseology, what I had told the man I had thought was the FBI. The tall and rigid man stood and heard me out, then reached for a phone. You are a spy, he said, I can recognize one of them at a hundred paces. I knew then that I had imagined all of this, both the FBI and the CIA, and that I was in no building, but on a gray and darkling plain that stretched flat in all directions to a far horizon that was gray itself, so that I had some difficulty in determining where the plain left off and the sky began.

"You ought to try to go to sleep," said Kathy. "You need the sleep. Do you want an aspirin?"

"No aspirin," I mumbled at her. "I haven't got a headache."

What I had, I knew, was far worse than a headache. It was no dream, for I was half awake. I knew all the time that these other things were running in my mind that I was in a car and that the car was moving. The landscape outside the car was not lost on me; I was aware of tree and hill, of field and far-off village, of the other cars upon the road and of the road shimmering out into the distance, of the sound of engine and of tires. But the awareness was a background awareness only, dimmed and dulled, a surface awareness that seemed to make no impact upon the visions summoned up by a brain that had lost its governor of reason and was running wild, summoning up the fantasy of the might-have-been.

I was back on the plain again and I saw now that it was featureless, a lonely and eternal place, that its flatness was not marred by any hill or ridge or tree, that it ran on forever in its utter sameness and that the sky, like the plain, also was featureless, without a cloud or sun or star and it was hard to tell whether it might be day or night—it was too light for night and too dark for day. It was a deep dusk and I wondered whether it might be always like this, a place where it was never anything but dusk, reaching toward the night, but never getting there. As I stood there on the plain, I heard the baying coming from far away, a sound that was unmistakable, the very sound that I had heard when I had stepped out for a breath of air and had heard the pack go crying down the notch of Lonesome Hollow. Frightened by the sound, I turned slowly, trying to determine from what direction it might come, and in my slow turning I caught sight of a thing that stumbled its way along the far horizon, its blackness dimly outlined against the grayness of the sky. Dim, but not to be mistaken, not that long sinuous neck which terminated in the ugly, darting, seeking head, not that serrated backbone.

I ran, although there was no place to run, certainly no place that one could hide. And as I ran I knew what sort of place it was, a place that had existed forever and would exist forever, where nothing had ever happened or was about to happen. Now there was another sound, a steady, oncoming sound that could be heard in the silences which lay between the baying of the wolves—a flapping, plopping sound that had an undertone of rustling and at times a harsh, hard buzzing. I spun about and searched the surface of the plain and in a little time I saw them, a squadron of humping, wriggling rattlesnakes bearing down upon me. I turned and ran, the air pumping in my lungs, and as I ran I knew there was no use of running and no need. For this was a place where nothing had ever happened and where nothing would ever happen and because of this it was a place of perfect safety. I ran, I knew, from nothing but my fear. It was a safe place, but by that very token, a place of futility and of hopelessness. But nevertheless I ran, for I could not stop the running. I heard the baying of the wolves, no closer and no farther off than they had been at first, and the slap, slap of the hunching rattlesnakes keeping pace with me. My strength ran out and my breath ran out and I fell, then got up and ran again and fell again. Finally I fell and lay there, not caring any more, not caring what might happen, although I knew that in this place nothing at all could happen. I didn't try to get up. I just lay there and let the hopelessness and the futility and the blackness close in upon me.

But suddenly I became aware that something had gone wrong. There was no motor hum, no hiss of rubber on the pavement, no sense of motion. There was, instead, the sound of a quiet wind blowing and the scent of many blossoms.

"Wake up, Horton," Kathy's startled voice said. "Something happened, very, very strange."

I opened my eyes and struggled upward. I lifted both my fists and scrubbed at sleep-smudged eyes.

The car had stopped and we were no longer on the highway. We were on no road at all, but on a rutted cart track that went wandering down a hill, dodging boulders and trees and brightly flowering shrubs. Grass grew between the deep wheelmarks and a wildness and a silence hung over everything.

We seemed to be on top of a high ridge or a mountain. The lower slope was heavily forested, but here, on top, the trees were scattered, although their size made up for the fewness of them—most of them great oaks, their mighty branches scarred and twisted, their boles spotted with heavy coats of lichens.

"I was just driving along," said Kathy, shaken, "not going too fast, not as fast as the highway limit—fifty more than likely. And then I was off the road and the car was rolling to a stop, its engine killed. And that's impossible. It couldn't happen that way."

I still was half asleep. I rubbed my eyes again, not so much to get the sleep out of them as because there was something wrong about the place.

"There was no sense of deceleration," Kathy said. "No

jolt. And how could one get off the highway? There's no way to leave the highway."

I'd seen those oaks somewhere before and I was trying to remember where I might have seen them—not the selfsame trees, of course, but others that were like them.

"Kathy," I asked, "where are we?"

"We must be on top of South Mountain. I'd just passed through Chambersburg."

"Yes," I said, remembering, "just short of Gettysburg." Although when I had asked the question, that had not been exactly what I'd meant.

"You don't realize what happened, Horton. We might have both been killed."

I shook my head. "Not killed. Not here."

"What do you mean?" she asked, irritated at me.

"Those oaks," I said. "Where have you seen those oaks before?"

"I've never seen . . ."

"Yes, you have," I said. "You must have. When you were a kid. In a book about King Arthur, or maybe Robin Hood."

She gasped and reached her hand out to my arm. "Those old romantic, pastoral drawings . . ."

"That is right," I said. "All oak trees in this land, most likely, are that kind of oaks, and all poplars tall and stately and all pine trees most triangular, as in a picture book."

Her hand tightened on my arm. "That other land. The place that friend of yours . . ."

"Perhaps," I said. "Perhaps."

For even knowing that it could be no other place, that if what Kathy said were true, we'd both be dead if it were not that other land, it still was a hard thing to accept.

"But I thought," said Kathy, "that it would be full of ghosts and goblins and other horrid things."

"Horrid things," I said. "Yes, I'd think you'd find them here. But more than likely some good things as well."

For if this were actually the place my old friend had hypothesized, then it held all the legends and the myths,

110

all the fairy tales that man had dreamed hard enough for them to become a part of him.

I opened the door of the car and stepped out.

The sky was blue—perhaps a shade too blue—a deep, intense and still very gentle blue. The grass was slightly greener, it seemed to me, than grass had the right to be, and yet in that extra-greenness there was a sense of gladness, the kind of feeling an eight-year-old boy might have in walking barefoot through the soft, new grass of spring.

Standing there and looking at it, I realized that the place was entirely storybook. In some subtle way that I could sense, but could not really name, it was not the old and solid earth, but a bit too perfect to be any place on Earth. It looked the way that painted illustrations looked.

Kathy came around the car to stand beside me.

"It's so peaceful here," she said. "You really can't believe it."

A dog came pacing up the hill toward us—pacing, not trotting. He was a crazy-looking dog. His ears were long and he tried to hold them upright, but the upper half of them folded over and hung down. He was big and ungainly and he carried his whiplike tail straight up in the air like a car antenna. He was smooth-coated and had big feet and was unbelievably skinny. He held his angular head high and he was grinning, with a fine display of teeth, and the funny thing about it was that they were human instead of canine teeth.

He moved up close to us and then stopped and stretched his front paws out on the ground and put his chin down on them. His rear end was elevated and his tail went round and round, revolving in a circle. He was very glad to see us.

Far down the slope someone whistled sharply and impatiently. The dog sprang to his feet, swinging around in the direction from which the whistle had come. The whistle sounded again and with an apologetic backward look at us, the caricature of a dog went swarming down the hill. He ran awkwardly, his back feet reaching forward to overlap his front feet, and his tail, canted at an angle of forty-five degrees, swung furiously in a circle of overwhelming happiness.

"I've seen that dog before," I said. "I know that I have seen him somewhere."

"Why," said Kathy, surprised at my nonrecognition, "it was Pluto. Mickey Mouse's dog."

I found that I was angry at myself for my stupidity. I should have recognized the dog immediately. But when one is all set to see a goblin or a fairy, he does not expect to have a cartoon character come popping out at him.

But the cartoon characters would be here, of course— the entire lot of them. Doc Yak and the Katzenjammer Kids, Harold Teen and Dagwood and, as well, all the fantastic Disney characters let loose upon my world.

Pluto had run up to see us and Mickey Mouse had whistled him away and we, the two of us, I thought, accepted it as a not unusual fact. If a man had stood off from this place, to one side of it, and had looked upon it in a logical, human manner, he never could have accepted it. Under no circumstances could he have admitted there was such a world or that he could be in it. But when he was there and could not stand aside, the doubt all dropped away, the zaniness rubbed off.

"Horton," Kathy asked, "what do we do now? Do you think the car could manage on that road?"

"We could take it slow," I said. "In low. And it might get better as we went along."

She walked around the car and got behind the wheel. She reached for the key and turned it and absolutely nothing happened. She switched it off and turned it once again and there was no sound, not even the clunking of a balky starter.

I walked around to the front of it, unlatched the hood and lifted it. I don't know why I bothered. I am no mechanic. There was nothing I possibly could have done to get at the trouble.

I leaned over the radiator and had a look at the motor and it looked all right to me. Half of it could have been missing and it still would have looked all right to me.

A gasp and a thump jerked me upright and I banged my head against the hood.

"Horton!" Kathy cried.

I stepped quickly to one side of the car and Kathy was sitting beside the road. Her face was twisted up in pain.

"My foot," she said.

Her left foot, I saw, was wedged tightly in a rut.

"I got out of the car," she said, "and stepped back, not looking where I stepped."

I knelt down beside her and worked her foot free as gently as I could, leaving the shoe jammed in the rut. Her ankle was red and bruised.

"What a stupid thing to do," she said.

"It hurts?"

"You're damned right it hurts. I think that it is sprained."

The ankle looked as if it might be sprained. And what in hell, I wondered, did one do with a sprained ankle in a place like this? There'd be no doctors, of course. I seemed to remember that you fixed a sprain with an elastic bandage, but there was no elastic bandage, either.

"We ought to get the stocking off," I said. "If it starts to swell . . ."

She hiked up her skirt and unfastened a garter, pushing the stocking down. I managed to work it down over the ankle and once it was off, there could be no doubt that the ankle was badly hurt. It was inflamed and there was some swelling.

"Kathy," I said, "I don't know what to do. If you have some idea . . ."

"It's probably not so bad," she said, "although it hurts. In a day or two it should be better. We have the car for shelter. Even if it won't run, it will be a place to stay."

"There might be someone who could help," I said. "I don't know what to do. If we had a bandage. I could rip up my shirt, but it should be an elastic . . ."

"Someone to help? In a place like this!"

"It's worth a try," I said. "It's not all ghouls and goblins. Perhaps not even many of them. They are out-of-date. There would be others . . ."

She nodded. "Perhaps you're right. That idea of using the car for shelter doesn't cover everything. We'll need food and water, too. But maybe we're getting scared too soon. Maybe I can walk."

"Who's getting scared?" I asked.

"Don't try to kid me," said Kathy, sharply. "You know we're in a jam. We know nothing about this place. We're foreigners. We have no right to be here."

"We didn't ask to come here."

"But that makes no difference, Horton."

And I don't suppose it did. Someone apparently wanted us to be here. Someone had brought us here.

Thinking about it, I grew a little cold. Not for myself—or, at least, I don't think for myself. Hell, I could face anything. After rattlesnakes, sea serpent, and werewolves, there was nothing that could faze me. But it wasn't fair for Kathy to be dragged into it.

"Look," I said, "if I got you in the car, you could lock the doors and I could take a short, fast look around."

She nodded. "If you'd help me."

I didn't help her. I simply picked her up and put her in the car. I eased her into the seat and reached across her to lock the opposite door.

"Roll up the window," I told her, "and lock the door. Yell if something shows up. I won't be far away."

She started to roll up the window, then rolled it down again, reaching down to the floor of the car. She came up with the baseball bat and stuck it through the window.

"Here, take this," she said.

I felt a little foolish going down the path with the bat in hand. But it made a good heft in my fist and it might be handy.

Where the path curved to go around the big oak I stopped and looked back. She was staring through the windshield and I waved at her and went on down the path.

The ground pitched sharply. Below me the forest closed in, dense and heavy. There was no breeze and the trees stood up motionless, the greenness of their leaves glinting in the sun of late afternoon.

I went on down the road and at a place where it twisted

again to dodge another tree, I found the signpost. It was old and weatherbeaten, but the legend still was clear. TO THE INN, it said, with an arrow pointing.

Back at the car, I told her, "I don't know what kind of inn, but it might be better than just staying here. There might be someone who could doctor up the ankle. At least we could get some cold water or some hot water—which is it you use to help a sprain?"

"I don't know," she said, "and I don't like the idea of an inn, but I suppose we can't stay sitting here. We have to get an idea of what is going on, what we should expect."

I didn't like the idea of an inn any better than she did—I didn't like anything that was going on; but what she said was right. We couldn't stay huddled on that hilltop and wait for whatever was about to happen.

So I got her out and perched her on the hood while I locked the door and pocketed the key. Then I picked her up and started down the hill.

"You forgot the bat," she said.

"There was no way to carry it."

"I could have carried it."

"More than likely we won't need it," I told her and went on down the road, picking my way as carefully as I could so I wouldn't stumble.

Just below the signpost, the road twisted again to make its way around a massive heap of boulders and as I rounded the boulders, there on the distant ridge was the castle. I stopped dead when I saw it, shocked into immobility by the unexpectedness of the sight.

Take all the beautiful, fancy, romantic, colorful paintings of castles that you have ever seen and roll them all together, combining all their good points. Forget everything you have ever read about a castle as a dirty, smelly, unsanitary, drafty habitation and substitute instead the castle of the fairy tale, King Arthur's Camelot, Walt Disney's castles. Do all of this and you might get some slight idea of what that castle looked like.

It was the stuff of dreams; it was the old romanticism and the chivalry come across the years. It sat upon the distant ridgetop in its gleaming whiteness, and the multicolored pennants mounted on its spires and turrets rippled in the air. It was such a perfect structure that one knew instinctively that there never could be another one quite like it.

"Horton," Kathy said, "will you put me down. I'd like to sit awhile and simply look at it. Did you know it was there all the time and you never said a word . . ."

"I didn't know it was there," I told her. "I came back when I saw the sign about the inn."

"We could go to the castle, maybe," she said. "Not the inn."

"We could try," I said. "There must be a road."

I put her down upon the ground and sat down beside her.

"I think the ankle may be getting better," she said. "I think that I could manage even if I had to walk a ways."

I took a look at it and shook my head. It was red and shiny and had swollen quite a lot.

"When I was a little girl," she said, "I thought castles were shining and romantic things. Then I took a couple of courses on the society of medieval days and I learned the truth about them. But here is a shining castle with all its pennons flying and . . ."

"It's the kind of place," I said, "that you thought about, the kind of castle that you and a million other little girls formed within their romantic little minds."

And it wasn't only castles, I reminded myself. Here in this land resided all the fantasies that mankind had developed through the centuries. Here, somewhere, Huckleberry Finn floated on his raft down a never-ending river. Somewhere in this world Red Ridinghood went tripping down a woodland path. Somewhere Mr. Magoo blundered along on his near-blind course through a series of illogical circumstances.

And what was the purpose of it, or did there have to be a purpose? Evolution was often a blind sort of operation, appearing on the surface to be of no great purpose. And humans, perhaps, should not attempt to find the purpose here, for humans were too entirely human to conceive, much less understand, any manner of existence other than their own. Exactly as the dinosaurs would have been incapable of accepting the idea (if dinosaurs ever had ideas) of the human intelligence which was to follow them.

But this was a world, I told myself, that was a part of the human mind. All things, all creatures, all ideas in this world or this dimension or this other place were the products of the human mind. This was, in all likelihood, an extension of the human mind, a place that took the thought the human mind had formed and used that thought as raw material by which a new world and a new evolutionary process had been fabricated.

"I could sit here all day," said Kathy, "and keep on looking at the castle, but I suppose that we should start if we ever are to get there. I don't think I can walk; do you mind a lot?"

"There was a time in Korea," I told her, "during a retreat, when my cameraman got it in the thigh and I had to carry him. We had stayed behind a bit too long and . . ."

She laughed at me happily. "He was much bigger," I told her, "and much less lovable and most dirty and profane. He showed no gratitude."

"I promise you my gratitude," she said. "It is so wonderful."

"Wonderful?" I asked, "with a busted ankle and in a place like this . . ."

"But the castle!" she cried. "I never thought I'd see a castle like that—the kind of castle I used to dream about."

"There is one thing," I said. "I'll say it once and I'll not mention it again. I am sorry, Kathy."

"Sorry? Because I got a busted ankle?"

"No, not that," I said. "Sorry that you're here at all. I shouldn't have let you mix into this. I never should have let you get the envelope. I never should have phoned you from that little place—from Woodman."

She crinkled up her face. "But there was nothing else that you could do. By the time you phoned, I had read the paper and I was involved. That was why you called."

"They might not have touched you, but once we were in the car, heading east for Washington . . ."

"Horton, pick me up," she said, "and let's be on our way. If we're late getting to the castle, they may not let us in."

"All right," I said. "The castle."

I got up and stooped to lift her, but as I did the brush rattled to one side of the path and a bear stepped out. He was walking upright and wore a pair of red shorts with white polka dots on them, held up by a single suspender looped across a shoulder. He carried a club across the other shoulder and he grinned most engagingly at us.

Kathy shrank back against me, but she didn't scream, although she had every right to, for this bear, despite his grin, had a look of disrepute about him.

Out of the brush behind him stepped a wolf, who carried no club and also tried to smile at us, but his smile was less engaging and somehow sinister. After the wolf came a fox and all three of them stood there in a row, grinning at us in right good fellowship.

"Mr. Bear," I said, "and Mr. Wolf and Br'er Fox. How are you today?"

I tried to keep my voice light and even, but I doubt that I succeeded, for I didn't like these three. I wished most earnestly I'd brought along the ball bat.

Mr. Bear made a little bow. "We are gratified," he said, "that you recognize us. And it is most fortunate we meet. I take it that the two of you are new to these environs."

"We have just arrived," said Kathy.

"Well, then," said Mr. Bear, "it is good we are well met. For we have been searching for a partner in a goodly undertaking."

"There is a chicken roost," said Br'er Fox, "that needs some looking into."

"I am sorry," I told them. "Maybe later on. Miss Adams has sprained her ankle and I must get her somewhere for medical attention."

"Now that is too bad," said Mr. Bear, trying to look sympathetic. "A sprained ankle, I would think, might be a

118

painful burden for anyone to carry. And especially for milady, who is so beautiful."

"But there is this chicken roost," said Br'er Fox, "and with evening comin' on . . ."

Mr. Bear rumbled throatily at him. "Br'er Fox, you have no soul. You have nothing but a stomach that is forever empty. The chicken roost, you see," he said to me, "is an adjunct to the castle and it is well guarded by a pack of hounds and various other carnivores and there is no hope for such as the three of us to gain entry to it. Which is a crying shame, for those hens have grown over-fat and would make toothsome eating. We had thought, perhaps, that if we could enlist a human we might sit down and work out a plan that had some promise of success. We have approached certain of them, but they are cowardly creatures, not to be depended on. Harold Teen and Dagwood and a great many others of them and they all are hopeless. We have a luxurious den not very far from here where we could sit down and evolve a plan. There would be a comfortable pallet for milady and one of us could go and fetch Old Meg with potions for the injured ankle."

"No, thank you," Kathy said. "We are going to the castle."

"You may be too late," said Br'er Fox. "They are overmeticulous with the closing of the gate."

"We must hurry, then," said Kathy.

I stooped to pick her up, but Mr. Bear reached out a paw and stopped me. "Surely," he said, "you are not about to dismiss with so little thought this matter of the chickens. You like chickens, do you not?"

"Of course he likes them," said the wolf, who had not spoken until now. "Man is as confirmed a carnivore as any one of us."

"But finicky," said Br'er Fox.

"Finicky," said Mr. Bear, aghast. "Those are the plumpest hens these old eyes have ever seen. They'd be finger-licking good and surely there could be no one who would want to pass them by."

"Some other time," I told them, "I'd view your proposition with overwhelming interest, but as of the moment we must be getting on."

"Some other time, perhaps," Mr. Bear said, bleakly.

"Yes, some other time," I said. "Please look me up again."

"When you are hungrier," Mr. Wolf suggested.

"That might make a difference," I admitted.

I lifted Kathy and held her cradled in my arms. For a moment I wasn't sure they would let us go, but they stepped aside and I went down the path.

Kathy shivered. "What terrible creatures," she said. "Standing there and grinning at us. Thinking we would join in their chicken thievery."

I wanted to look back, to be sure they were still there and not stalking along behind us. But I didn't dare to look, for it would have made them think I was afraid of them. I was afraid of them, but that made it all the more important that I not show it.

Kathy put her arms around my neck and hung on with her head against my shoulder. It was much more satisfactory, I told myself, carrying her than that benighted, foul-mouthed cameraman. And, besides, she didn't weigh as much.

By now the path had led off the fairly open ridgetop into deep and stately woods and only on occasion could I see the castle through some accidental woodland vista and then only portions of it. The sun was falling close to the western horizon and the depths of the woods were filled with smoky twilight and in their shaded recesses I became aware of many furtive stirrings.

The path forked and became two and there was another signpost, with two pointing arrows this time, one pointing to the castle, the other to the inn. But just a few yards down the path leading to the castle a massive iron gate barred any further progress, and stretching out on either side of it was a high fence of heavy steel mesh, with barbed wire on top of it. A gaily striped kiosk stood to one side of the gate and a man-at-arms leaned against it with a halberd held very sloppily. I walked up to the gate and

120

had to kick it to attract his attention.

"Ye be late," he growled. "The gate is closed at sunset and the dragons are let loose. It would be worth your life to go a furlong down that road."

He came to the gate and peered closer at us.

"You have a damsel with you. Is she in distress?"

"Her ankle's hurt," I said. "She cannot walk."

He sniggered. "If such be the case," he said, "it might be arranged to provide escort for the damsel."

"For both of us," said Kathy, sharply.

He wagged his head in mock sadness. "I stretch the point to let one past. I cannot stretch for both."

"Someday," I said, "it will not be a point but your neck that will be stretched."

"Begone!" he shouted, angrily. "Begone and take your slut along. At the inn, the witch will mutter spells to mend the ankle."

"Let's get out of here," said Kathy, frightened.

"My friend," I said to the man-at-arms, "I shall make a point, when I am less encumbered, of coming back and raising lumps on you."

"Please," said Kathy. "Please, let's get out of here!"

I turned around and left. Behind us, the man-at-arms roared threats and banged the gate bars with his halberd. I turned down the path that led to the inn and once out of sight of the castle gate stopped and let Kathy to the ground, crouching down beside her.

She was crying, more with anger, it seemed to me, than with fear.

"No one," she said, "has ever called me a slut."

I did not point out to her that manners and language of that sort sometimes went with castles.

She raised her arm and pulled my head down close beside her face. "If it hadn't been for me," she said, "you could have clobbered him."

"That was all talk," I told her. "There was a gate between us and he had that fancy stabber."

"He said there was a witch down at the inn," she said.

I turned my head and kissed her gently on the cheek.

"Are you trying to take my mind off witches?"

"I thought it might help," I said.

"And there was that fence," she said. "A wire fence. Who ever heard of a fence around a castle? Back in those days they hadn't even invented wire."

"It's getting dark," I said. "We'd better head for the inn."

"But the witch!"

I laughed, not that I really felt like laughing. "Mostly," I told her, "witches are just old eccentric women no one understands."

"Maybe you are right," she said.

I lifted her and got on my feet.

She held up her face and I kissed her upon the mouth. Her arms tightened about me and I held her body close, feeling the warmth and the sweetness of her. For a long moment there was nothing in the empty universe but the two of us and it was only slowly that I came back to a realization of the darkening woods and of the furtive stirrings in it.

A short way down the path I saw a faint rectangle of light that I knew must be the inn.

"We're almost there," I told her.

"I won't be any bother, Horton," she promised. "I'll not do any screaming. No matter what there is, I'll never scream."

"I'm sure you won't," I said. "And we'll get out of here. I don't know exactly how, but somehow we'll make it out of here, the two of us together."

Seen dimly in the deepening dark, the inn was an old ramshackle building, huddled beneath a grove of towering, twisted oaks. Smoke plumed from the chimney in the center of the roofline and the feeble window-light shone through diamond panes of glass. The inn yard was deserted and there seemed no one about. Which was just as well, I told myself.

I'd almost gotten to the doorway when a bent, misshapen figure moved into it, a black, featureless body outlined by the dim light from inside.

"Come on in, laddie," shrilled the bent-over creature.

"Don't stand gawping there. There is naught to harm you. Nor milady, either."

"Milady has sprained her ankle," I said. "We had hoped . . ."

"Of course," the creature cried. "You've come to the most likely place to have a job of healing. Old Meg will stir up a posset for it."

I could see her somewhat more clearly now and there could be no doubt that she was the witch of which the man-at-arms had told us. Her hair hung in wispy, ragged strands about her face and her nose was long and hooked, reaching for an upcurved chin and almost reaching it. She leaned heavily upon a wooden staff.

She stepped back and I moved through the door. A fire that blazed smokily upon the hearth did little to relieve the darkness of the room. The smell of wood smoke mingled with and sharpened the other undefinable odors that lay like a fog upon the place.

"Over there," said Meg, the witch, pointing with her staff. "The chair over by the fire. It is of good construction, made of honest oak and shaped to fit the body, with a wool sack for a seat. Milady will be comfortable."

I carried Kathy over to the chair and lowered her into it.

"All right?" I asked.

She looked up at me and her eyes were shining softly in the firelight.

"All right," she said, and her words were happy.

"We're halfway home," I told her.

The witch went hobbling past us, thumping her staff upon the floor and muttering to herself. She crouched beside the fire and began stirring a pan of steaming liquid set upon the coals. The firelight, flaring up, showed the ugliness of her, the incredible nose and chin, the enormous wart upon one cheek, sprouting hairs that looked like spider legs.

Now that my eyes were becoming accustomed to the darkness, I began to make out some of the details of the room. Three rough plank tables stood along the front wall and unlighted candles, set in candlesticks upon the tables, leaned askew like pale and drunken ghosts. A large hutch cabinet at one end of the room held mugs and bottles that glinted faintly in the stuttering firelight flickering in the room.

"Now," said the witch, "just a bit of powdered toad and a pinch of graveyard dust and the posset will be finished. And once we fix the damsel's ankle, then there will be food. Aye, yes, there will be food."

She cackled shrilly at a joke I could only guess at—something about the food, perhaps.

From some distance off came the sound of voices. Other travelers, I wondered, heading for the inn? A company of them, perhaps.

The voices grew louder and I stepped to the door to look in the direction from which they came. Coming up the track, climbing the hill, were a number of people and some of them were carrying flaring torches.

Behind the crowd came two men riding horses, but as I watched the procession, I saw after a little time that the one who rode behind the other rode a donkey, not a horse, with his feet almost dragging on the ground. But it was the man who rode in front who attracted my attention and very well he might. He loomed tall and gaunt and was dressed in armor, with a shield upon one arm and a long lance carried on one shoulder. The horse was as gaunt as he was and it walked with a stumbling gait and with its head held low. As the procession approached closer I saw, in the light cast by the torches, that the horse was little better than a bag of bones.

The procession halted and the people parted as the horse carrying the tall scarecrow in armor stumbled through the crowd and to the front. Having walked clear of the crowd, it halted and stood with hanging head and I would not have been surprised if, at any moment, it had fallen in a heap.

Man and horse held motionless and the crowd as well and watching them warily, I wondered rather vaguely what might happen next. In a place like this, I knew, it could be anything. The whole thing was ridiculous, of course—but that was no consolation, for it was a judgment based on the manners and the mores of the human

124

twentieth century and it was not valid here.

The horse slowly raised his head. The crowd shuffled expectantly, with the torches bobbing. And the knight, with what seemed a conscious effort, straightened and stiffened himself in the saddle and brought down the lance. I stood there, in the innyard, an interested spectator and just a bit befuddled as to what it might be all about.

Suddenly the knight was shouting and, although his voice rang out loud and clear in the silence of the night, it took an instant for me to sort out what he said. The lance, braced against his thigh, had leveled, and the horse had launched itself into a gallop before I realized the intent of his words.

"Catiff," he had shouted, "wretch, dirty infidel, make ready to defend thyself!"

And it must have been me he meant, I gathered, because the horse was thundering toward me and the lance was pointed at me and, God knows, I had no time at all to prepare for my defense.

If there had been time, I'd have taken to my heels, for I knew I was outclassed. But I didn't have the time to do anything at all and I was, in fact, half frozen by the craziness of it and in the few intervening seconds that somehow seemed like hours I stood and watched in fascination as the glittering lance point came bearing down upon me. The horse was no great shakes, but he was good for a sudden burst of speed and he was thundering along like an asthmatic locomotive.

The lance point was only a few feet away and about to spit me when I came alive enough to move. I jumped backward. The point went past me, but as it did the knight seemed to lose control of it, or the horse might have shied or stumbled—I don't know which it was—but, in any case, the lance swung sharply toward me and, reaching out my hands, I batted at it blindly to shove it away from me.

I hit it and deflected it downward and the point plunged into the ground. Suddenly the lance, its point deeply buried, became a catapult so that its butt, catching in the armpit of the knight, hoisted him off the saddle and high into the air. The horse dug in its feet and skidded to a halt, with the stirrups swinging wildly, while the bowed lance straightened and hurled the hapless knight like a rock fired from a slingshot. He arched through the air and landed, face downward and spread-eagled, at the far end of the yard and when he hit the ground there was a clangor such as one might make if he hit an empty steel drum a resounding lick with a heavy hammer.

Up the road the people who had formed the procession for the knight were convulsed with glee. Some of them were doubled over, laughing, with their arms wrapped about their middles, while others of them were rolling on the ground, helpless with their guffaws.

Shambling down the road came the lop-eared little donkey, still carrying the tattered man whose feet almost dragged upon the ground—poor, patient Sancho Panza coming once again to the relief of his master, Don Quixote de la Mancha.

And those others rolling in the road, I knew, had merely come along for the fun of it, willingly bearing torches to light the way for this scarecrow knight, knowing very well that one of his never-ending misadventures would sometime in the not-too-distant future provide amusement for them.

I turned away, back toward the inn—and there wasn't any inn.

"Kathy!" I shouted. "Kathy!"

There was no answer. Up the road the amusement-seeking company still was howling out its laughter. At the far end of what had been the inn yard Sancho had dismounted from the donkey and was trying manfully, but with small success, to roll Don Quixote over on his back. But the inn was gone and there was no sign of either Kathy or the witch.

From somewhere in the woods and down the slope came the shrill cackling of the witch. I waited and the cackle came again and this time I pinpointed the direction and went plunging down the slope. I crossed the few feet of cleared space that had served as the inn yard and ran into the woods. Roots clutched at my toes, seeking to trip me up, and branches raked my face. But I kept on run-

126

ning, with my arms outstretched to protect me against running into a tree headfirst and beating out what little brains I had. Ahead of me the insane cackling still went on.

If I could only catch her, I promised myself, I'd wring her scrawny neck until she took me to Kathy or told me where she was, and after that the temptation, I knew, would be great to continue with the wringing. But I knew even then, I think, how little chance I had of catching her. I banged into a boulder and fell across it and felt my way around it and went on running down the slope, while ahead of me, leading me on, never any farther off, never any closer, the crazy laughter still went on. I ran into a tree, but my outstretched hands found it first and saved me from a cracked skull, although I thought for a moment that both the wrists were fractured. And, finally, one of the roots on the forest floor managed to trip me up and I went cartwheeling through the air, but I landed soft—in the edge of a woodland swamp. I landed on my back and my head went under and I sat up coughing and retching, for I had swallowed some of the foul swamp water.

I sat there, without stirring, knowing I was licked. I could chase that cackle through the woods for a million years and not lay hands upon the witch. For this was a world, I knew, with which neither I, nor any other human, could cope. A human would be dealing with the fantasies he'd hatched and all his worlds of logic would not come up with any answers.

I sat in the mud and water to my waist and above my head the cattails swayed and off to my left something—I suppose a frog—went jumping through the muck. Dimly I became aware of a light glowing faintly off to the right of me and I got up slowly. Mud fell off my trousers with little, sodden plops as it hit the water. But, even standing, I could not see the light well, for I sank close to my knees in muck and the cattail growth came up around my head.

With some difficulty, I began to make my way toward the light. It was not easy going. The muck was deep and sticky and the cattails, mixed with water-loving bushes, helped to impede my progress. I plodded forward slowly, forcing my way through the heavy growth.

The mud and water became shallower and the cattail growth began thinning out. I saw that the light was shining from a point somewhere above my head and I wondered where that light might be, but a moment later, when I came to a sloping bank, I knew the light was atop the bank. I started to climb the bank, but it was slippery. Part-way up, I started skidding back and as I did, a great brawny hand came out of nowhere and I grabbed at it and felt the fingers of it close hard around my wrist.

I looked up and saw the thing that the hand belonged to, leaning down from the bank, with his arm out-stretched. The horns were there, set upon his forehead and his face was a heavy face, coarse in texture but with a foxy look despite the coarseness of the features. His white teeth flashed at me in a sudden grin and for the first time since it all had started, I think that I was scared.

And that wasn't all. There, perched upon the edge of the bank beside him, was a squatty thing with a pointed head and when it saw that I had seen it, it began hopping wrathfully.

"No! No!" it screamed. "Not two! Just one! Quixote doesn't count!"

The Devil gave a jerk and hauled me up the bank in a single motion and set me on my feet.

A lantern was set upon the ground and by its light I could see that the Devil was a chunky character, a bit shorter than I was, but built most powerfully and running to a lot of fat. He wore no clothes except a dirty loincloth tied about his middle and his overgrown paunch hung across it in a fold.

The Referee kept on with his squeaky squawling. "It is not fair," he shouted. "You know it is not fair. That Quix-ote is a fool. He never does things right. The beating of Dox Quixote is no facing of a danger and . . ."

The Devil turned and swung his foot, the cloven hoof flashing in the lantern light. The kick caught the Referee somewhere in his middle and hoisted him and sent him sailing out of sight. His squawling trailed off into a reedy sound and ended in a splash.

"There now," said the Devil, turning back to me, "that

will give us a moment of honest peace and quiet, although he is a most persistent pest and will be crawling out to pester us again. It doesn't seem to me," he said, switching quickly to another subject, "that you appear too frightened."

"I'm petrified," I said.

"It is something of a problem," the Devil complained, switching his barbed tail back and forth to show his puzzlement, "to know just how one should appear when he confronts a mortal. When you humans persist in portraying me in so many different guises, one can never know which of them is the most effective. As a matter of fact, I can assume any one of the many forms which are attributed to me if you have a preference. Although I must confess that the one in which you see me now is, by all odds, the most comfortable to carry."

"I have no preference," I said. "Continue in your comfort." I was getting back some courage, but I still was shaky. It's not every day one converses with the Devil.

"You mean, perhaps," he said, "that you've not spent much thought on me."

"I guess that's it," I said.

"That is what I thought," he answered, dolefully. "That has been the story of my life in the last half-century or so. People almost never think of me and when they do they aren't scared of me. Oh, a bit uncomfortable, perhaps, but not really scared. And that is hard to take. Once upon a time, not too long ago, the entire Christian world was plenty scared of me."

"There may be some who still are," I told him, trying to comfort him. "In some of the backward countries, they must still be scared of you." And as soon as I'd said it, I was sorry that I had, for I could see that it was no comfort to him, but only made him feel the worse.

The Referee came clambering up the bank. He was covered with mud and his thatch of hair was dripping, but when he reached the top, he went into a wild war dance of rage. "I will not have it," he shouted at the Devil. "I don't care what you say. He still has two to go. You cannot deny the werewolves, but you must deny Quixote, who is

129

no fit antagonist. I tell you the Rule will go for nothing if
. . ."

The Devil sighed in resignation and reached out to grip
my arm. "Leave us go," he said, "to some place where we
can sit and talk."

There was a mighty swish and a peal of sudden thunder
and a smell of sulphur in the air and, in the space of one
short breath, we were otherwhere, upon a rise of cleared
ground that rose above a swale. We were standing near a
clump of trees and beside the trees lay a heap of tumbled
boulders. From the swale below us came the peaceful
croaking of happy, springtime frogs and a little breeze was
rustling the trees. All in all, it was a much more inviting
place than the bank beside the swamp.

My knees were buckling under me, but the Devil held
me up and led me to the boulders and there he sat me
down upon one of the boulders that proved very comfortable. Then he sat down beside me, crossed one leg
over the other and curled his spiked tail around until the
end of it rested in his lap.

"Now," he said, "we can converse without undue
disturbance. The Referee may hunt us out, of course, but
it will take some time. I pride myself, beyond all others,
upon my mastery of the art of going elsewhere very
rapidly."

"Before we settle down to any lengthy conversation," I
told him, "there are some questions that I want to ask.
There was a woman with me and she has disappeared. She
was at the inn and . . ."

"I know all that," he told me, with a leer. "Name of
Kathy Adams. You can rest easy concerning her, for she
has been returned to Earth—the human Earth, that is.
Which is just as well, for we didn't want her. But we had
to take her, because she was with you."

"Didn't want her?"

"No, of course not," the Devil said. "You were the one
we wanted."

"Now, look here . . ." I started to say, but he cut me off
with an airy wave of a massive hand.

"We need you as a negotiator. I suppose that's the way

to say it. We've been looking for someone who could do a job for us, you might say be our agent, and then you came along and . . ."

"If that was what you wanted," I told him, "you went about it in a ham-handed sort of way. Your gang did their best to kill me and it was only by good luck . . ."

He interrupted me with a chuckle. "Not good luck," he said. "A well-honed sense of self-preservation that worked far better than anything I've seen for years. And about this business of trying to do you in—I can promise you that there are certain expediters here who have smarted for it. They have one-track minds and too much imagination and there'll be some changes made. I was busy with too many other things, as you can well imagine, and did not hear, at first, of what was going on."

"You mean that this rule of three times is a charm . . ."

He shook his head sadly. "No, I regret to tell you there is nothing I can do to change that. A rule's a rule, you know. And, after all, it was you humans who made up the rule along with a bunch of others that made no sort of sense. Like 'Crime does not pay,' when you know damn well it does, and all that foolishness about early to bed and early to rise." He shook his head again. "You can't begin to imagine the kinds of trouble those fool rules of yours are always giving us."

"But they aren't rules," I said.

"I know. You call them adages. But once you get enough people to believe there is something in them, then we are stuck with them."

"So you are still going to have one more go at me. Unless you agree with the Referee that this Quixote business . . ."

"The Quixote business stands," he growled. "I agree with the Referee that this crack-brained character out of Spain is not difficult for anyone above the age of five to handle. But I want you out of this and the quicker and the easier I can get you out of it, the better it will be. There's business to be done. What I can't understand is what misplaced sense of chivalry made you agree to take on another round. Once you polished off the serpent, you were in the clear, but then you let that slimy Referee talk you into . . ."

"I owed Kathy something," I told him. "I got her into it."

"I know," he said. "I know. There are times I can't get you humans figured out. Most of the time you go around slitting one another's throats and sticking knives into your fellow humans' backs and climbing over them to achieve what you call success, then you turn around and get so damn noble and compassionate it's enough to make one sick."

"But why, in the first place, if you had some use for me, and I really can't believe you have—but if you do, why try to kill me? Why not just reach down, if that is how you do it, and simply pick me up?"

He sighed at my ignorance. "To kill you we must try. That also is a rule. But there was no need for so good a job of it. No need for all the fancy business. These expediters sit around and think up these fancy schemes, and it's all right if that's the way they like to spend their time, but they get so hopped up about these fancy ways of doing it, that they have to try them out. The trouble they will go to to accomplish simple homicide is past all understanding. It's all you humans' fault, of course. You humans do the same. Your book writers, your comic artists, your script writers—every one of your creative people—sit around and think up all these crazy characters and these impossible situations and we are the ones who get stuck with them. And that, I think, brings us around to the proposition I wish to talk with you about."

"Then get on with it," I said. "I've had a tough day and could do with about twenty hours of sleep. That is, if there is a place where I can bed down."

"Oh, there is," he said. "In between those two boulders over there is a bed of leaves. Blown in by the winds of latest autumn. It will be a restful place to catch a needed nap."

"Complete," I asked, "with rattlesnakes?"

"What do you take me for?" the Devil demanded,

wrathfully. "Do you think I have no honor, that I would entrap you? I pledge to you that no harm will come to you before you're well awake."

"And after that," I asked.

"After that," he said, "there is yet another threat and danger to fulfill the rule of three. You can rest assured that you have my best wishes in that encounter, whatever it may be."

"O.K.," I said, "since I can't weasel out of it. I wonder if you might just speak a word for me. I'm getting slightly worn down. I don't think I'd care right now for another serpent."

"I can promise you," the Devil said, "it won't be a serpent. And now let's get down to business."

"All right," I told him, somewhat weakly. "What is on your mind?"

"It is," the Devil said, somewhat petulantly, "this junky fantasy that you are feeding us. How do you expect us to build any kind of life system with all this fuzziness and froth? Little dicky birds perching on a branch and yelling 'I thought I saw a putty tat—I did, I did, I did,' and the fool cat down there on the ground leering up at the bird in a helpless and half-guilty manner. Where, I ask you with wholesome honesty, can we arrive at any decent character in a situation such as this? You gave us, to start with, a foundation that was solid and substantial, born out of firm conviction and a sound belief. But now you are facetious, and you give us character patterns that are both improbable and weak, and material such as this, rather than contributing to our strength, is undermining all we have accomplished in the past."

"You mean," I said, "that it would be a more healthful setup for you if we continued to believe in devils, ghouls, and goblins, and such-like."

"Much more healthful," said the Devil, "at least if you believed with some sincerity. But now you make a joke of us . . ."

"Not a joke," I protested. "You must remember that, for the most part, the human race is not aware that any of

133

you actually exist. How could they be when you go about killing off the ones who have some suspicion that this world exists?"

"It is this thing," said the Devil, bitterly, "that you designate as progress. You can do almost anything you want and you keep on wanting more and you fill your minds with hopeful expectations and have no room for introspection on personal values—such as one's own shortcomings. There is no fear in you and no apprehension . . ."

"There is fear," I said, "and plenty of apprehension. The difference is in the things we fear."

"You are right," the Devil said. "The H-bombs and the UFO's. What a thing to conjure up—crazy flying saucers!"

"Better, perhaps, than a devil," I reminded him. "A UFO a man might have some chance to reason with, but a devil, never. You kind of folks are tricky."

"It's the sign of the times," the Devil mourned. "Mechanics instead of metaphysics. Would you believe that in this sad land of ours we have a horde of UFO's, most detestable contrivances and inhabited by all manner of most horrendous aliens. But with no honesty in their horror such as I carry in my person. Gimmicky creatures that make no sort of sense."

"Perhaps it's bad for you," I told him, "and I can see your point. But I don't know what can be done about it. Except in certain culturally backward areas you find few people now who believe in you with any honesty. Oh, sure, they talk of you at times. They say 'to the devil with it' or that it's the devil's work, but mostly they don't even think of you when they are saying it. You've become a very faintly dirty word. The belief in you simply isn't there. Not the way it once was. I don't think that attitude can be changed. You can't stop human progress. You'll simply have to wait for what comes next. It might just possibly be something that will work to your advantage."

"I think we can do something," the Devil said, "and we're not about to wait. We've waited too long now."

"I can't imagine what you'd do," I said. "You can't
. . ."

"I am not about to reveal my plans to you," he said.
"You are by far too clever, with that dirty, weasely,
ruthless cleverness of which only a human being can be
capable. I tell you this much only so that sometime in the
future you will understand and then perhaps will find
some willingness to act as an agent for us."

And, saying this, he vanished in a puff of sulfurous
smoke and I was left alone upon the ridgetop, the smoke
of his leaving drifting eastward with the wind. I shivered
in the wind, although it wasn't really cold. The coldness
was, rather, from the company I'd been keeping.

The land was empty, lighted palely by the moon
—empty and silent and foreboding.

He had said there'd be a bed of leaves between two
boulders and I hunted for and found it. I poked around in
it, but there were no rattlesnakes. I hadn't thought there'd
be; the Devil didn't seem the kind of being who'd tell a
downright lie. I crawled between the boulders and arranged the leaves so I'd be more comfortable.

Lying there in the darkness, with the wind moaning on
the land, I thought, with thankfulness, of Kathy safely
home. I'd told her that somehow we would make it back,
the two of us together, and when I'd told her that I had
not dreamed that within another hour she would be safely
home. Through no effort of my own, of course, but that
didn't really matter. It had been the Devil's doing and although his act had not been dictated by compassion, I
found myself feeling rather kindly toward him.

I thought of Kathy, her face turned up toward me in the
firelight from the blaze upon the witch's hearth, and I
tried to catch again the happiness that had been upon her
face. I couldn't seem to get the right expression and while
I still was trying I must have gone to sleep.

To wake to Gettysburg.

14

Something nudged me and woke me so quickly that I sat bolt upright and bumped my head on one of the boulders. Through the stars that spun within my brain I saw a man scrooched down and staring at me. He held a rifle and while the barrel was aimed in my direction, I got the impression that he wasn't really pointing it at me. He had used it, more than likely, to nudge me into wakefulness.

He wore a forage cap which did not fit well because it had been some time since he had had a haircut, and his jacket was a faded blue with brass buttons on it.

"It do beat all," he said, amiably, "how some folk can fall asleep just any time at all."

He turned his head aside and spat a neat stream of tobacco juice onto the face of one of the boulders.

"What's going on?" I asked.

"The Rebs are bringing up their guns," he said. "All morning they been at it. They must have a thousand of them, on the rise across the way. Lined up, hub to hub."

I shook my head. "Not a thousand of them. Two hundred would be closer to it."

"Mebbe you are right," he said. "I guess them Rebs ain't got no thousand guns."

"This must be Gettysburg," I said.

"Of course it's Gettysburg," he said, disgusted. "Don't tell me you don't know. You couldn't have been here long without knowing what it is. There've been right smart doings here, I tell you, and if I don't miss my guess, we'uns are going to start catching hell again in just a little while."

It was Gettysburg, of course. It simply had to be. There had been, I recalled, a fleeting familiarity to the grove of trees the night before—last night, I thought; had it been last night, or a century before last night? In this world did time make as little sense as all the rest of it?

I crouched on the bed of leaves and tried to get my bearings. Last night a grove of trees and a clump of boulders and this morning Gettysburg!

I bent my head and crawled out from between the boulders, but stayed squatting to face the man who'd wakened me. He shifted the quid from one cheek to the other and looked me over closely.

"What outfit are you with?" he asked, suspiciously. "I don't recollect no one rigged out the way you are."

If I had been a bit more alert, perhaps I could have found an answer, but my mind still was fogged with sleep and my skull still hurt from the knock upon the boulder. Waking up at Gettysburg hadn't helped me, either. I knew that I should answer, but there was no answer I could think of, so I simply shook my head.

On the summit of the slope above me, cannons were ranged in line, with the cannoneers beside them, standing stiff and straight, staring out across the swale that lay below the ridge. A field officer sat erect upon a horse that was prancing nervously, while on the slope below the cannon the infantry lay sprawled in a long, uneven line, some of them behind barricades variously constructed, some of them flat upon the ground, while others sat around at leisure, all staring off across the swale.

"I don't like it," said the soldier who had found me. "I don't like the looks or smell of it. If you are from the town, you ain't got no business up here."

From far off came a heavy bang, sonorous, but not very loud. At the sound, I stood up and looked across the swale and could see that from the tree line on the opposite ridge a puff of smoke was drifting up. Further down the line of trees there was a sudden flash, as if someone had opened the door of a red-hot stove, then closed it immediately.

"Get down!" the soldier was yelling at me. "Get down, you goddamn fool . . ."

The rest of what he said was blotted out by a jarring crash from somewhere just behind me.

I saw that he was flat upon the ground and so were all the others. I threw myself heavily, sprawling. Another crash sounded to my left and then I saw the sparkling of many stove doors opening along the other ridge. From the air above and ahead of the ridge on which I lay came the sound of whickering objects traveling very fast, and then, on the ridge behind me, the entire world blew up.

And kept on blowing up.

Beneath me the very ground was bucking with the cannonade. The air thundered until it was unendurable and kept on being unendurable. Smoke drifted across the heaving ground and as a sort of undertone to the crashing of the shot and shell were whirring, whistling noises. With that utter clarity of thought which sometimes comes when one is stiff with fear, I realized that the whistling was made by chunks of metal flying off the ridge behind me and spraying down the slope.

With my face pressed tight against the ground, I twisted my head so that I could have a look back at the ridgetop. I was surprised to find there wasn't really much to see—certainly not what I had expected seeing. A heavy fog bank of smoke obscured the entire ridge, hanging not more than three feet above the ground. Below the smoke I saw the legs of frantic gunners as they worked their battery of guns, as if a group of half-men were firing a battery of half-guns, with only a little better than a half of the carriages showing, the rest obscured by roiling smoke.

Out of that roiling smoke came stabbing bursts of fire as the hidden guns fired back across the swale. At each belch of flame, I felt an angry flare of heat sweep through the air above me, but the uncanny thing about it was that the barking of those cannons firing directly over me was so muffled by the racket of the bombardment which swept the ridge that it sounded as if they were being fired from some distance off.

Through the cloud bank of smoke, and above it, the shells were bursting, but the bursts, dimmed by the smoke, were not the quick, bright flashes of light one would have expected them to be, but twinkling spurts of red-orange flame that ran along the ridge like a flashing neon sign. A huge explosion sent a flare of brilliant red flashing through the smoke and a massive volcano of black smoke went surging upward through the gray cloud bank. One of the plunging shells had found a caisson.

I huddled closer against the ground, doing my best to burrow into it, to press myself so flat and make myself so heavy that my weight would dent the ground and thus offer me protection. I remembered, as I huddled there, that I probably was in one of the safest spots on all of Cemetery Ridge, for on that day more than a century ago the Confederate gunners had been aiming high, with the result that the worst of the bombardment fell, not on the ridge itself, but on the reverse slope of the ridge.

I twisted my head around to its original position and looked across the swale and over on Seminary Ridge another cloud of smoke was boiling above the treetops, while near the base of the cloud ran tiny flickerings, marking the mouths of the Confederate cannons. I had said two hundred to the soldier who had spoken to me and now I recalled that it had been a hundred and eighty and that on the ridge behind me were eighty others replying to that hundred eighty—eighty-odd, the books had said. And that it now must be somewhat after one o'clock, for the cannonade had started at shortly after one and had continued for two hours or so.

Over there, somewhere, General Lee sat on Traveller and watched. Over there, somewhere, Longstreet sat glumly on a rough rail fence, pondering his conviction that the charge which he must order would surely fail its purpose. For this kind of charge, he figured, was the Yankee way of making war and that the South's best hope had always been a stubborn defense, luring the Union forces into attack and holding hard against them and wearing down their strength.

But, I told myself, my thinking held a flaw. There was no Lee or Longstreet over on that other ridge. The battle that had been fought on this ground had been fought more than a century ago and would not be fought again. And this mock battle which here was being staged would not be a re-enactment of the battle as it had been really fought, but a playing over of the tradition of it, of the way in which later generations had imagined it had been fought.

A chunk of iron plunged into the ground just ahead of me, tearing up the turf. I reached out a cautious hand to touch it, but jerked it back before I touched it, for the iron was hot. And that chunk of iron, I felt very sure, if it had hit me, could have killed me as easily and effectively as if this had been an actual battle.

Over to my right was the small grove of trees where the Confederate charge had reached highwater mark and then had dwindled away, back down the slope again, and back of me and also to the right, but now concealed by cannon smoke, were the great ugly cemetery gates. The country looked, I had no doubt, as it had looked that day more than a century ago and this re-enactment of the battle would adhere to the timetables, so far as they could be known, and the movements of specific regiments and smaller military groups, and all the rest of it, but there would be much that would be lost, the little details that later generations did not know or glossed over in preference to really knowing them—all the things that Civil War round tables, meeting once a month for dinner and discussion, might know for a certainty or might suspect were right, would be here re-enacted, but one would not find here the things that no man could have known without having lived through the actual battle.

The pandemonium went on and on and did not let up—the clangor and the pounding and the hammering, the dust and smoke and flame. I clung tightly to the ground that seemed to keep on heaving underneath me. I could no longer hear and in time it seemed that I had never heard and would never hear again, but there had never been such a thing as hearing, that I had imagined it.

To either side of me and out in front of me, the blue-clad bodies also hugged the ground, crouched behind boulders, snuggling closely against piled-up fence rails, cowering in shallow and hastily dug pits, behind stone walls, keeping their heads down, clutching rifles that

141

pointed up and outward toward the hill where the Confederate cannon spouted. Waiting for that time when the cannon stopped and the long line of marching men, walking like troops upon parade, should come tramping across the swale and up the hill.

How long had it been going on? I wondered. I twisted my wrist up in front of my face and it was eleven thirty and that was wrong, of course, for the cannonade had not started until one o'clock at least, and probably some minutes after that. It was the first time I had thought to look at my watch since I had been pitchforked into this stupid land and there was no way of knowing how time here might compare with time on earth, or if, even, this place had such a thing as time.

I decided that perhaps it had been no more than fifteen or twenty minutes since the cannonade had started—although it seemed much longer, which was only natural. In any case, I was certain I had a long time yet to wait before the guns ceased firing. So I settled down to it, making sure that I presented as small a target as was possible. Having decided that all I could do was to wait it out, I began to worry about what I'd do when the cannonade had ended and the Confederate line came tearing up that final slope, with the red battle flags snapping in the wind and the sun glinting off the bayonets and sabers. What would I do, I wondered, if one of them came lunging at me with a bayonet? Run, of course, if there were anywhere to run—and there'd probably be plenty of others running as well, but more than likely there'd be blue-clad officers and men back across the ridge who'd take a very dim view of anyone fleeing headlong from the battle. There was no question of trying to defend myself, even if I could get my hands upon a gun, for those guns were the most awkward-looking things a man had ever seen, and as far as firing one of them, I'd have no idea whatsoever how to go about it. All of them seemed to be muzzle-loaders and I knew less than nothing about that kind of weapon.

The battle fog was growing thicker, blotting out the sun. The swale was filled with drifting smoke and a layer of smoke floated only a short distance above the heads of the men who crouched upon the slope in front of the belching Union batteries. Looking down the hill, it seemed to me that I was looking down a narrow slot that was hedged in by a flapping curtain of very dirty gray.

Far down the slope something was stirring—not a human being, smaller than a human. A small dog, I thought, caught between the lines, although it was too brown and furry and didn't look quite like a dog. A woodchuck, more than likely. And I told him: Chuck, if I were you, I'd pop back into my den and stay there for a while. I don't think I really spoke to him, although even if I had, it would have made no difference, for no one, let alone that screwy woodchuck, ever would have heard me.

He kept on sitting there for a while, then he started moving up the slope toward me, pushing through the pasture grass.

A swirl of smoke dipped down in front of me and blotted out the woodchuck. Behind me the battery still was firing, with the guns going chuff-chuff instead of speaking out, the customary bellow of them muted by the overriding scream and crash of the avalanche of exploding metal pouring through the sky. Bits of metal at times came pattering down, like heavy raindrops falling from the smoke cloud, and occasionally a bigger fragment went tearing along the sod, ripping out and throwing tiny gobs of dirt into the air.

The swirl of smoke cleared away. The woodchuck was much closer now and I saw that it was no woodchuck. How I could have failed to distinguish immediately that pointed thatch of hair, the juglike ears, I will never know. Even at a distance I should have been able to know that the Referee was not a woodchuck or a dog.

But now I could see him clearly and he was looking straight at me, daring me, challenging me, like a defiant bantam rooster, and as I watched him, he lifted one splayfingered hand and deliberately thumbed his nose at me.

I should have had more sense. I should have let him go. I should have paid no attention to him. But the sight of him, standing there, bandy-legged and cocky, thumbing his nose at me, was more than I could bear.

143

Without thinking, I surged upward, raging at him. I took one step down the slope before whatever it was that hit me, hit me. I don't remember too much, just a little of it. A red-hot iron that glanced along my skull, a sudden dizziness, a sense of falling down the slope, falling very fast, and that was all there was.

15

It seemed that I had been climbing for a long time, through an abandoned land of darkness, although I kept my eyes squeezed shut and could not truly know that it was dark. But it seemed to me it was, it seemed to me I could feel the darkness through my skin, and I speculated upon how silly I would feel if, opening my eyes, I should open them to the noonday sun. But I did not open them. For some compelling reason about which I had no sense of sureness, it seemed that I must keep them closed—almost as if somewhere just beyond me was a sight which no mortal was allowed to see. But that was pure fantasy. I had no fact to make me think that it was so. Perhaps the most terrible thing about it all was that I had no facts, that I existed in a dark world where there were no facts, and that I crawled through an empty land—not merely an empty land, but one in which, until a short time ago, there had been much solid substance and a great deal of vital life, but that now had been emptied of all its life and matter.

I kept on climbing, crawling up the slope, painfully and slowly, not knowing where I might be going or why I might be going there. And it seemed to me that in doing this I was quite content—not because it was a thing that I wished to do, but because the alternatives to doing it were so horrible as to be beyond my comprehension. I had no recollection of who I was or what I was or how I'd come to be there, or any idea of when I'd started on this climb; it seemed, in fact, that I had been always climbing in the darkness up this endless slope.

But now, as I crawled, new things came to me—the feel of the ground and the grass beneath my hands, the uneasy pain of a small rock that caught and scraped my knee, the slight, cooling pressure of a small wind against one side of my face, and a fluttering sound—the sound of that same wind moving through leaves somewhere above my head. And that was more than there had been before. This world, I thought, this dark place, had come to life again. I quit my crawling and lay flat against the earth and could sense the stored heat of the summer afternoon being given up by it. Then more than the wind moving through the leaves broke the stillness—the stumbling tramp of feet, the sound of distant voices.

So I opened my eyes and it was dark, as I imagined it had been, but not as dark as I had thought it might be. Just beyond me stood a small clump of trees and on the ridge just beyond the trees, in silhouette against the star-strewn sky, stood a drunken cannon, with a wheel caved in and the muzzle of the barrel tilted toward the stars.

Seeing this, I remembered Gettysburg and from where I lay I knew I had not been doing any crawling. I was in the same place, or approximately the same place, I had been that afternoon when I had lurched to my feet as the Referee had thumbed his nose at me. The only crawling I had done had been in the feverish confusion of my mind.

I put a hand up to my head and found that a thick, greasy scab had formed on one side of my skull. When I took my hand away I could feel the stickiness of my fingers. I struggled up onto my knees and stayed kneeling there a moment to take stock of myself. The side of my head, where I had touched it, was sore, but my mind seemed clear—I felt no fuzziness, no wooziness. And I seemed strong enough. A splinter of iron had barely touched me, I reasoned, breaking skin and peeling away some of the hair.

The Referee, I realized, had almost accomplished what he had intended and I was alive by the slightest fraction of an inch. Had the battle been fought, I wondered, for my sole benefit, for my entrapment only? Or was it something that went on at periodic intervals, a regularly scheduled show played out again and yet again, fated to be played out unendingly so long as the people on my earth showed interest and concern in Gettysburg?

I got to my feet and my legs were strong beneath me, although I had a most strange feeling in the middle of me, and as I stood there wondering about it, I realized that the strange feeling was no more than the simple one of hunger. The last time I had eaten had been the day before when Kathy and I had stopped for lunch just short of the Pennsylvania line. My yesterday, of course—I had no way of knowing how time ran here on this shattered hillside. The bombardment, I remembered, had started at least two hours too soon by the watch upon my wrist, although there was no general historical agreement as to the precise moment it had started. But certainly not before one o'clock. But that was something, I told myself, that probably had little bearing upon the situation here. In this lopsided world, the curtain could go up at any time the stage manager might wish.

I started walking up the hill and after no more than three strides my foot caught against something lying on the ground and I pitched forward across it, putting out my hands to catch myself so that I didn't fall flat upon my face. I got two fists full of gravel when I fell, but that wasn't the worst of it. The worst of it was when I twisted around to find out what I had fallen over. And as I gagged at the thought of it, I saw that there were others of them, a great many others of them scattered here where the two lines of contending men had met and fought it out and now were no more than loglike lumps, lying peacefully in the dark, with the slight wind fluttering tag ends of their clothing, perhaps to remind one they once had been alive.

Men, I thought—but, no, not men. Nothing for one to grieve over except, perhaps, in remembrance of another time when all of this had been for real and not a stupid dumb-show.

A different form of life, my old friend had speculated. A better form of life, perhaps. A development that was one of the points of significance in the continuing evolutionary process. The force of thought, perhaps. The substance of abstract thought here snared and shaped and made to live and die (or pretend to be dead) and then, in turn, to become a simple force again and again to be shaped and formed and made to live again, either in its present form or in another form.

It made no sense, I told myself. But, then, nothing ever had made any sense. Fire had made no sense until a now unknown man had tamed it. A wheel had made no sense until someone dreamed it up. Atoms had made no sense until inquiring minds envisioned them and proved them (without actually understanding them) and atomic energy had made no sense until a strange fire had been lit at the University of Chicago and, later, a towering, fierce mushroom had blossomed in the desert.

If evolution were, as it seemed, a continuing process to bring about a life force which could live with, or cope with, its environment, then here, in such a flexible, malleable life form evolution must surely be close to a final achievement and a final glory. For here would be a life form which, because it was not essentially matter, but could become, theoretically at least, any form of matter, was able to adapt itself automatically to any environment, fit itself into any ecology.

But what was the sense of it, I asked myself, lying there upon the field of Gettysburg, with the dead men (dead men?) at my feet. Although, come to think of it, it might be far too early to be seeking for a purpose. The naked carnivorous ape that roamed Africa in hunting packs two million years, or more, ago, if he could have been observed by some intelligence, would have seemed to have far less purpose than the strange beings of this world.

I pushed myself to my feet again and went on up the slope, past the clump of trees, past the shattered cannon—and now I saw that there were many shattered cannons—until I reached the ridgetop and could look down the reverse slope.

The stage still was set, I saw. Campfires sparkled down the slope and south and east and from far off came the janglings of harness and the creaking sound of wagons on

148

the move, or perhaps artillery. Down toward the Round Tops a mule began to bray.

Over all hung the brilliance of the summer stars, and this, I recalled, was a misreading of the script, for after that final charge up the fated slope there had been heavy rain and some of the wounded, helpless to move themselves, had been caught by a rising creek and drowned. It had been "cannon weather." So often had great storms followed on the heels of bitter battle that men in the ranks believed the rains were caused by heavy cannonading.

The near hillside was dotted by the dark, humped shapes of dead men and occasionally a dead horse, but there seemed to be no wounded, nor was there the sound of wounded, that pitiful moaning and crying that went on after every battle, sometimes punctuated by the unnerving shrieks of those few men who screamed. Surely, I told myself, all the wounded could not have been found and carried off by this time, and I wondered if there ever had been any wounded—if, perhaps, the script of fact and history might not have been edited and cleaned up a bit by the elimination of the wounded.

Looking at those dim figures humped upon the ground, I sensed the quiet and peace of them, the majesty of death. None lay distorted, all were decently composed, as if they might simply have lain down and gone to sleep. There was in them no agony and no pain. Even the horses were horses that had gone to sleep. None lay with bodies bloated by the gas of death, with legs outthrust grotesquely. The entire battlefield was polite and neat and orderly and, perhaps, a touch romantic. There was editing here, I knew, but not so much the editing of this world as the editing of mine. This had been the way the people who had lived at the time of Gettysburg had thought about this war, the way later generations also had thought of it after the years had stripped it of its harshness and brutality and horror, and had draped across it a chivalrous mantle, making of it a saga rather than a war.

I knew that it was wrong. I knew that this was not the way that it had been. But, standing there, I half forgot

149

that it was nothing but a play and could only feel the gold-spangled glory and the glory-haunted melancholy.

The mule had quit his braying and somewhere a group about a campfire had begun to sing. Behind me the leaves were whispering in the clump of trees.

Gettysburg, I thought. I had been here in another time, on another world (or in another world, or of another world, whatever it might be, or however it worked out) and had stood, on this very spot, and tried to imagine what it had been like, and now I saw—or, at least, I saw a part of it.

I started down the hill when a voice spoke my name.

"Horton Smith."

I swung toward the sound and for a moment I failed to see the one who had spoken, and then I did, perched upon the broken wheel of the shell-smashed cannon. I could see just the outline of him, the thatched and pointed head, the juglike ears, and, for once, he was not bouncing in consuming rage; he was simply roosting there.

"So it's you again," I said.

"You had the Devil's help," said the Referee. "You did not do it fair. The encounter with Quixote should not count at all and you must have needed the Devil's help to live through the cannonade."

"All right. So I had the Devil's help. What do you do about it?"

"You admit it?" he asked, eagerly. "You admit that you had help?"

"Not at all," I said. "You said it and I don't really know. The Devil said nothing to me about giving any help."

He slumped, dejected. "Ah, then there is nothing one can do. Three times is a charm. It is the law and I cannot question it, although," he said, sharply, "I would like to very much. I do not like you, Mr. Smith. I like you not at all."

"It's a feeling," I told him, "that I reciprocate."

"Six times!" he mourned. "It is immoral! It is impossible! There has never been anyone before who even did it three times."

150

I walked close to the cannon where he perched and took a good hard look at him. "If you can find any comfort in it," I finally told him, "I made no deal with the Devil. I asked him to speak a kind word for me, but he indicated that he couldn't do it. He said a rule was a rule and there was nothing he could do."

"Comfort!" he shrilled, puffing up in rage. "Why should you wish to give me comfort? It's another trick, I tell you. Another dirty human trick!"

I turned abruptly on my heel. "Go chase yourself," I told him. What was the use of trying to be civil with a jerk like that?

"Mr. Smith," he called after me. "Mr. Smith. Please, Mr. Smith."

I paid him no attention and went on, tramping down the hill.

To my left I saw the faint outlines of a white farmhouse, enclosed by a picket fence which was white as well. Some of the fence, I saw, had been torn down. Light shone through the windows and tied horses stamped in the yard outside the house. That would be General Meade's headquarters and the general might be there. If I wanted to walk over, I might get a glimpse of him. But I didn't walk over. I kept on down the hill. For the thing that was Meade would not be really Meade, no more than the house was really a house or the broken cannon a cannon. It was all cruel make-believe, but in a very solid form—a form so solid that for a moment, back there on the hilltop, I'd caught the sense of a substantial and historic battlefield.

Now there were hidden voices all about me and occasionally the sound of footsteps and at times I caught the sight of dim human figures hurrying across the hill, on official business, perhaps, but more than likely on business of their own.

The ground beneath my feet plunged sharply and I saw that it led down into a gulch, with a thicket of small trees at the upper end of it. Beneath the trees was the flare of a campfire light. I tried to veer away, for I had no wish to meet anyone, but I had gone too far to avoid detection.

Small stones loosened by my feet went rolling and bouncing down into the gulch and a voice cried out sharply at me.

I stopped and stood stock-still.

"Who's there?" the voice cried again.

"Friend," I said, and it was a silly thing to say, but all that I could think of.

The firelight glinted on a lifted musket barrel.

"There ain't no need, Jed, to be so upset," said a drawling voice. "There ain't no Rebs around and even if there were, they'd be inclined to be plumb peaceful."

"I just wanted to make sure, is all," said Jed. "After today, I ain't taking any chances."

"Take it easy," I said, walking toward the fire. "I'm not any Reb."

I stopped when I was in sight of them and let them look me over. There were three of them, two sitting by the fire, the other on his feet with the musket lifted.

"You ain't one of us, neither," said the standing one, who apparently was Jed. "Just who are you, mister?"

"My name is Horton Smith," I said. "A newspaper-man."

"Well, what do you know," said the one who drawled. "Come on in and sit by the fire with us for a spell if you have got the time."

"I have some time," I said.

"We can tell you all about it," said the one who had not spoken before. "We was right up there in the thick of it. Right by the clump of trees."

"Wait a minute," said the drawly one. "We don't need to tell him. I seen this gentleman before. He was up there with us for a while. Maybe all the time. I seen him, then things got hot and I lost track of everything."

I walked toward the blaze. Jed leaned his musket against a small plum tree and resumed his seat beside the fire.

"We was frying up some sow belly," he said, motioning toward the pan set on a bed of coals raked out from the fire. "If you are hungry, we got plenty of it."

"But you got to be hungry," said one of the others, "or you can't nohow stomach it."

"I think I'm hungry enough," I said. I came into the circle of the firelight and squatted down. Beside the pan of frying pork sat a steaming coffee pot. I sniffed at its aroma. "It seems that I missed lunch," I said, "and breakfast, too."

"Then maybe you can manage it," said Jed. "We got a couple of extra hardtack and I'll make you up a sandwich."

"Be sure," said the drawling one, "to knock them against something to dislodge the crawlers. Someone that ain't use to it might not like fresh meat."

"Say, mister," said the third one, "looks to me as if you picked up a crease."

I put my hand to my head and the fingers came away sticky.

"Knocked out for a while," I said. "Just came to a while ago. Shell fragment, I suppose."

"Mike," Jed said to the drawly one, "why don't you and Asa wash him up a bit and see how bad it is. I'll pour him a cup of coffee. Probably he could use it."

"It's all right," I said. "It is just a scratch."

"Better have a look," said Mike, "then, when you leave, head down to Taneytown Road. Just south on the road a piece you'll find a sawbones. He can slop some junk on it, keep it from mortifying."

Jed handed me a cup of coffee and it was strong and hot. I took a sip of it and burned my tongue. Mike worked on my head, as tenderly as if he'd been a woman, daubing away with a handkerchief soaked in water from his canteen.

"It's just a crease," he said. "Took off some hide, is all. But if I was you, I'd see me a sawbones."

"All right, I will," I said.

And the funny thing about it, I realized, was that these three men around their fire really believed that they were Union soldiers. There was no playacting here. They were what they were supposed to be. Perhaps they could be

153

anything at all, or the force (if it was a force) that could be shaped into form and matter, could be anything at all. But once that form had been taken, they were, to all intents and purposes, the thing that had been formed. In a little time, perhaps, their solid shapes would be transformed back to its elemental form, available then for another form and being, but until that came about they were Union soldiers who had just fought a battle on this shell-scarred hillside.

"It's all that I can do," said Mike, going back and sitting down. "I haven't even got a clean rag I can wrap around your head. But you find the doc and he'll fix you up."

"Here's a sandwich," said Jed, handing it to me. "I tried to knock the skippers out. I think I got the most of them."

It was an unappetizing-looking mess and the hardtack was as hard as I had read it was, but I was hungry and it was food and I put it down. Jed fixed sandwiches for the others and we all sat munching, not talking because it took a man's full concentration to eat that kind of food. The coffee had cooled enough so that I could drink it and it helped to wash the hardtack down.

Finally we were finished and Jed poured each of us another cup of coffee; Mike got out an old pipe and hunted around in a pocket until he found some crumbled shreds of tobacco with which to load the pipe. He lit it with a brand pulled gingerly from the fire.

"A newspaperman," he said. "From New York, most likely."

I shook my head. New York was too close. One of them might just happen to know a newsman from New York. "London," I said. "The *Times*."

"You don't sound like no Britisher to me," said Asa. "They got a funny way of talking."

"I haven't been in England for years," I said. "I've knocked around a lot."

It didn't explain, of course, how a man could lose his British accent, but it held them for the moment.

"There's a Britisher with Lee's army," Jed said.

"Freemantle or some such name as that. I suppose you know him."

"I've heard of him," I said. "I've never met the man."

They were getting just a bit too curious. Friendly still, of course, but too curious. But they didn't follow it up. There were too many other things they wanted to talk about.

"When you write your piece," asked Mike, "what do you intend to say of Meade?"

"Why, I don't really know," I said. "I haven't thought that much about it. He fought a splendid battle here, of course. He made the Southerners come to him. He played their game for once. A strong defense and . . ."

Jed spat. "That may all be so," he said. "But he hasn't got no style. Now Mac—there's a man who really had some style."

"Style, sure," said Asa, "but he was always letting us get licked. It feels right good, I tell you, to be on the winning side for once." He looked across the fire at me. "You think we won this one, don't you?"

"I'm sure of it," I said. "Lee will be pulling out tomorrow. Maybe he's pulling out right now."

"Some of the men don't think so," said Mike. "I was talking to some of the Minnesota troops. They figure them crazy Rebs will make another try."

"I don't think so," said Jed. "We broke their backs this afternoon. Hell's fire, they came walking up that hill as if they were on parade. They walked right up to us; they walked right into the cannon's mouth. And us blasting away at them the way you'd blast away at targets. We're always being told what a smart general this Lee is, but I tell you there ain't no general smart who will march his men up a pasture slope into the cannon's mouth."

"Burnside did it at Fredericksburg," said Asa.

Jed spat. "Burnside wasn't smart. No one ever said he was."

I finished my coffee, swirled the little that was left in the bottom of the cup to stir up the grounds, and tossed it at the fire. Jed reached out and lifted the pot.

"No more, thanks," I said. "I must be getting on."

I didn't want to be getting on. I wanted to stay right where I was and yarn away another hour or so with the three around the fire. The blaze was comfortable and the gully snug.

But I had a deep, underlying hunch that I had best get out when I could. Get away from these men and this battlefield before something else could happen. That bit of flying iron had been close enough. Theoretically, of course, I was in the clear, but I had no confidence in this land, nor in the Referee. The quicker out the better.

I rose to my feet. "Thanks for the food and coffee. It was something that I needed."

"Where you going now?"

"I think, first of all, I'll hunt up that doctor."

Jed nodded. "I would if I were you," he said.

I turned about and walked away, expecting each second that they would call me back. But they didn't and I went stumbling down the gully in the dark.

I had a crude, half-remembered map in mind and as I walked I figured out what I would do. Not the Taneytown Road that would keep me to close to the battlefield. I'd cross the Taneytown Road and keep on the east until I hit the Baltimore Pike and I'd follow that southeast. Although just why I bothered, I don't know. One place probably was as good as another in this weird place. I wasn't going anywhere, actually; I was just moving around. The Devil had said that Kathy was safe, back in the human world again, but there had been no hint from him as to how a man could get back into the human world and I wasn't downright sure that I could believe what the Devil said of Kathy. He was a shifty critter and not one to be trusted.

I reached the end of the gully and came out in a valley. Ahead of me lay the Taneytown Road. There were campfires here and there and I veered around them. But stumbling through the dark, I fetched up against a warm body that had hair and that snorted at me. I backed away and, squinting, made out it was a horse, tied to a still-standing section of a small rail fence.

The horse slanted its ears forward and nickered softly

156

at me. It probably had been standing there a long time and it may have been frightened and I got the feeling that it was glad to see a human being. It wore a saddle and was tied to the fence by a bridle rein.

"Hi, horse," I said. "Howsa fellow?"

It whuffled at me and I walked up and stroked its neck. It swung its head around and tried to nuzzle me.

I stepped back and had a look around and there was no one near. So I untied the reins and got them over the horse's neck and straightened out, then rather awkwardly climbed into the saddle. The horse seemed pleased to be untied and swung obediently as I reined it.

There was a tangle of wagons on the Taneytown Road, but I managed to get through them without anyone hailing me and once clear of the road, I headed the horse southeast and he took off at an easy lope.

We met small groups of men, plodding off somewhere, and had to swing around a battery of guns, but gradually the traffic cleared and the horse finally reached the Baltimore Pike and we went pounding down it, away from Gettysburg.

16

A few miles out of Gettysburg the road came to an end, as I should have known it would, for back there on South Mountain, where Kathy and I had landed in this place, there had been only a cart track and nothing like a road. The Pike and Taneytown Road and all the other roads, perhaps even Gettysburg itself, had been no more than a stage setting for the battle, and once one left the battle area, there was no need of roads.

Once the road gave out, I gave up any attempt to pick a route and let the horse go as it pleased. There was really no point to keeping on at all. There was no place I had in mind to go, but I let the horse keep on. For some reason, it seemed that it might be a good idea to build up a little distance.

Riding under the stars, in soft summer weather, I had the first chance since I'd come into the land to try to do some thinking. I reviewed in my mind all that had happened since I'd turned off the freeway onto the winding road that led to Pilot Knob and I asked a lot of questions about all the things that had happened after that, but there seemed no ready answers. When that became apparent, I realized that I was searching for answers that would serve my human logic and I knew that was a fruitless search. In the face of all I knew, there was no reason to believe that human logic had a thing to do with what was going on. I admitted to myself that the only possible explanation must be based upon the speculation in my old friend's manuscript.

Therefore there was a place, and I was in it, where the

force-substance (a very awkward term) of imagination became the basic stuff from which matter, or a semblance of matter, or a new concept of matter, might be formed. I worked for quite a while to work out a statement which would cover the situation, to reduce the *maybe*'s and the *if*'s to a workable proportion, but it was a hopeless job and, finally, for working purposes, I labeled this place that I was in the Land of Imagination and let it go at that. It was a cowardly way to do it, but maybe later on someone could work out a definition for it.

So here was this land, forged of all the fantasy, all the make-believe, all the fairy tales and folk stories, all the fictions and traditions of the race of Man. And in this land stalked and lurked and ran all the creatures and all the situations the ever-busy minds of all the flighty little primates had ever given birth. Here (on any night, or just on Christmas Eve?) Santa Claus went storming through the skies in his reindeer-drawn sleigh. Here, somewhere (on any night, or only of a Hallowe'en?) Ichabod Crane whipped his jaded mount down a rocky road in a desperate effort to reach a magic bridge before the Headless Horseman could hurl the pumpkin that hung at his saddlehorn. Here Daniel Boone stalked Kentucky meadows with his long rifle slung across his arm. Here the Sandman roamed and foul and grinning things danced jigs upon the ridgepole. And here the battle of Gettysburg was fought (again and yet again, or only for special purposes?), but not the battle as it had been fought, but fought in the polite and glorious and almost bloodless fashion in which the public mind in later years had conceived of its being fought. And other battles, too, perhaps, the great and bloody battles that loomed large in significance and larger in tradition. Waterloo and Marathon, Shiloh, Concord Bridge and Austerlitz, and in the days to come, when they'd become embedded in tradition, the mindless and mechanical and humanly agonizing battles of World Wars I and II, or Korea and Vietnam. In other years, as well, the fabulous Roaring Twenties, with the raccoon coats, the hip flasks and the flappers, the Stutz Bearcat and the gangsters, with machine guns comfortably ensconced in violin cases, would become a part of this land as well—perhaps already were.

All of these, all that man could think of or had thought of long enough—all the madness and the wit, all the buffoonery and the viciousness, all the lightness and the sadness which all men, in all ages, from the cave up to the present moment, had fashioned in their minds were in this very place.

It was madness, surely, when viewed in the cold light of human logic, but there it was, all around me. I rode through a landscape that was not the kind of landscape that one would find on earth, but a fairy landscape frosted by the starlight that came from stars among which was not recognizable a single one of the constellations that one saw on the human earth. A land of the impossible, where silly saws were laws, where there could be no such thing as logic since it all was built of imagination, which knew no kind of logic.

The horse kept on going, taking it at a walk where the going was uncertain, loping along quite smartly when the way was clear. My head ached a little and when I put my hand up to the wound, my fingers still were sticky, but a scab, I could feel, was beginning to form and it seemed that everything was all right. Otherwise, I felt better than I had imagined that I might and I rode along content, through the frosty landscape, beneath the glitter of the stars.

I expected that at any moment we might meet some of the strange denizens of this fantastic land, but none of them showed up. The horse finally struck a trail somewhat better traveled than the one he had been following and settled down into a lope. The miles went spinning out behind me and the air grew somewhat chilly. At times, far in the distance, I saw occasional habitations that were difficult to recognize, although one of them looked a good deal like a palisaded fort, the kind of place that the westward-trending pioneers had built when they'd shoved for the new lands of Kentucky. At times distant lights glowed through the star-struck darkness, but there was no way of telling what the lights might signify.

161

Suddenly the horse came to a jarring stop and it was only by sheer luck that I didn't keep on going, sailing straight above his head. He had been loping along, unconcernedly, like a contented rocking horse, and his halt came without warning, a stiff-legged skidding to a stop. His ears were slanted forward and his nostrils flared, as if he might be searching for something in the dark ahead.

Then he screamed in terror and leaped sidewise off the path, pivoting on his hind legs and heading at a frenzied gallop straight into the woods. I stayed on his back only by throwing myself upon his neck and grabbing at his mane and it was well I did, for there were occasional low branches that certainly would have brained me if I'd been upright in the saddle.

His senses must have been considerably sharper than mine, for it was not until he was off the path and running in the woods that I heard the mewling sound that ended with a slobber and caught a hint of the carrion odor that rode along the wind, while back of us there were crashing, crunching sounds, as if some huge, ungainly, terrible body was making its rapid way along the direction of our flight.

Hanging desperately to the horse's mane, I stole a brief glance backward and saw, out of the corner of one eye, the sickly greenness of some sort of shape that floundered in our wake.

Then, so quickly that I had no inkling of it until after it had happened, the horse was gone out from under me. He went out from under me as if he'd never been there and I fell straight down, landing first upon my feet, then falling backward and skidding on my bottom through the forest loam for a dozen feet or so before I shot out over the lip of a declivity and went rolling to its foot. I was shaken up and battered somewhat superficially, but I was able to stagger to my feet and face the cloud of sickly green that was plowing through the woods behind me.

I knew exactly what had happened and I should have expected it and been ready for it, but it had seemed so commonplace and ordinary, riding on the horse, that I'd never thought of the probability that at any moment the re-enactment of Gettysburg would come to an end. And now it had come to an end and back on those ridges and on the round-topped hills the still-living men and the huddled bodies scattered on the field, the shattered cannon, the now-spent cannon balls, the battle flags and all the other things that had been formed and gathered for the battle had simply disappeared. The play was over and the actors and the scenery had been whisked away and since the horse I had been riding had been a part of it, he'd also been whisked away.

I was left alone in this little sloping valley that ran through the woods to face the revolting greenishness that was raging on my trail—green in color and green, too, in the terrible smell of rottenness that went ahead of it. It was mewling more fiercely now and between the sounds of mewling were the sounds of slobbering and an eerie chittering that grated on my soul and as I stood there, facing back toward it, I finally knew exactly what it was—the creature dreamed by Lovecraft, the ravener of the world, the thing out of the Cthulhu mythos, the Old One that had been barred from Earth and now was back again, festering with a ghoulish, hideous hunger that would strip more than mere flesh from off the bones, that would numb the soul and life and mind of the one it captured with a nameless horror.

I felt the horror—I felt the hairs rising on my nape and my guts were churning and there was a sickness in me that made me somewhat less than human; but there was an anger, too, and it was the anger, I am sure, that kept me sane. That goddamned Referee, I thought, that dirty little double-crossing stinker! He hated me, of course—he had a right to hate me, for I had beaten him not only once, but twice, and I had turned my back and walked away from him, contemptuously, while he, squatting on the wheel of the ruined cannon, had tried to call me back. But rules were rules, I told myself, and I'd played those rules the way that he had called them and now I should, by right, be beyond all jeopardy.

The greenish light was brighter now—a deathly, sickly green—but as yet I could not make out the actual shape of the thing that followed me. The charnel-house odor was thicker and it clotted in my throat and filled my nostrils and I tried to gag, but couldn't, and of all of it, the smell was worst.

Then, quite suddenly, I saw the shape that came at me through the trees—not clearly, for the blackness of the tree trunks broke up the shape and fragmented it. But I saw enough to last me all my days. Take a swollen, monstrous toad, throw in a bit of spitting lizard, add something from a snake and you'll get a small idea, a very faint idea. It was much worse than that; it was beyond description.

Choking and gagging, water-legged with fear, I turned to run and as I turned the ground lurched under me and threw me forward on my face. I landed on some hard surface and my face and hands were skinned and there was a tooth that felt as if it had been loosened by the impact.

But the smell was gone and there was more light than there had been before and it was not a greenish light and when I scrambled up I saw there was no forest.

The surface I had fallen on, I saw, was concrete, and a sudden fear went knifing through my mind. An airport runway? A superhighway?

I stood staring groggily down the long lane of concrete.

I was standing squarely in the center of a highway. But there was no danger. No cars were roaring down upon me. There were cars, of course, but they weren't moving. They were just sitting there.

17

For quite some time I didn't realize what had happened.
First I had been frightened at the idea of standing out in
the middle of a high-speed highway. I recognized what it
was immediately—the broad lanes of concrete, the grassy
median separating them, the heavy steel fence snaking
along the right of way, closing off the lanes. Then I saw
the stranded cars and that was something of a jolt. An occasional car, parked on the shoulder, off the concrete, and
with its hood up, was not too unusual. But to see a dozen
or more of them in this condition was something else
again. There were no people, nor any signs of people.
There simply were the cars, some of them with their hoods
up, but not all of them. As if, suddenly, all these cars had
ceased to function and had rolled to a stop upon the highway. And it was not only the cars in my immediate
vicinity, but all up and down the lanes, as far as I could
see, were other standing cars, some of them no more than
black dots in the distance.

It was not until then, not until I had taken in and mentally digested the fact of the stranded cars, that the more
obvious fact hit me—the realization that should have
come immediately.

I was back on the human earth again! I was no longer
in that strange world of Don Quixote and the Devil!

If I'd not been so flustered by the cars, I suppose I
would have been most happy. But the cars bothered me so
much that they took the edge off any other kind of feeling
that I had.

I walked over to the nearest car and had a look at it.
An AAA travel map and a handful of other travel

literature lay on the front seat and a vacuum bottle and a sweater were tucked into one corner of the rear seat. A pipe sat in the ash tray and the keys were gone from the ignition lock.

I looked at some of the other cars. A few of them had some baggage left in them, as if the people might have left to seek out help and intended coming back.

By now the sun had risen well above the horizon and the morning was growing warm.

Far down the road an overpass, a thin line blurred by the distance, arched over the highway. Down there, more than likely, was an interchange that would get me off the highway. I started walking toward it and I walked in morning silence. A few birds flew among the groups of trees beyond the fence, but they were silent birds.

So I was home again, I thought, and so was Kathy, if one could believe the Devil. And where would she be? I wondered. More than likely in Gettysburg, safely home again. As soon as I reached a phone, I promised myself, I'd put in a call and check on her whereabouts.

I passed a number of stranded cars, but I didn't bother with them. The important thing was to get off the highway and find someone who could tell me what was going on. I came upon a signpost that said 70S and when I saw it, I knew where I was, somewhere in Maryland between Frederick and Washington. The horse, I realized, had covered a fair piece of ground during the night—that is, if the geography of that other world was the same as this one.

The sign pointing to the exit gave the name of a town of which I'd never heard. I trudged up the exit lane and where it joined a narrow road stood a service station, but the doors were locked and the place seemed to be deserted. A short distance down the road I came to the outskirts of a small town. Cars stood at the curbs, but there was no moving traffic. I turned in at the first place I came to, a small café built of concrete blocks painted a sickly yellow.

No customers were seated at the lunch counter running down the center of the building, but from somewhere in the back came a clatter of pans. A fire burned beneath an

166

urn back of the counter and the place was filled with the smell of coffee.

I sat down on a stool and almost immediately a rather dowdy woman came out of the back.

"Good morning, sir," she said. "You're an early riser."

She picked up a cup and filled it at the urn, set it down in front of me.

"What else will you have?" she asked.

"Some bacon and eggs," I said, "and if you'll give me some change, I'll use the telephone while you are cooking them."

"I'll give you the change," she said, "but it won't do you any good. The telephone's not working."

"You mean it's out of order. Maybe some other place, nearby . . ."

"No, that ain't what I mean," she said. "No telephones are working. They haven't worked for two days now, since the cars stopped running."

"I saw the cars . . ."

"There ain't nothing working," said the woman. "I don't know what will become of us. No radio, no television. No cars, no telephones. What will we do when we run short of food? I can get eggs and chickens from some of the farmers, but my boy, he has to go on his bicycle to pick them up and that's all right, because school is at an end. But what will I do when I run out of coffee and sugar and flour and a lot of other things? There aren't any trucks. They stopped, just like the cars."

"You are sure?" I asked. "About all the cars, I mean. You're sure they've stopped running everywhere?"

"I ain't sure of nothing," said the woman. "All that I know is I ain't seen a car go by in the last two days."

"You're sure of that, though?"

"I'm sure of that," she said. "Now I'll go and get your breakfast cooking."

Was this, I wondered, this thing that had happened, what the Devil had meant when he had told me he had a plan? Sitting atop Cemetery Ridge, he had made it sound as if it were no more than a plan that he was formulating when, in fact, it already had been put into operation.

Perhaps it had been initiated at that very moment when Kathy's car had left the turnpike and had entered into the shadow world of man's imagination. The other cars on the highway had rolled to a stop, but Kathy's car had been shunted to the cart track atop the mountain. When Kathy had tried to start it later, I recalled, it had refused to start.

But how could such a thing be done? How could all the cars be made to cease to operate, rolling to a stop, and then impossible to start?

Enchantment, I told myself; enchantment, more than likely. Although, just thinking of it, the idea seemed impossible.

Impossible, certainly, in the world in which I sat, waiting for the woman in the kitchen to cook my breakfast for me. But probably not impossible in the Devil's world, where enchantment would stand as a principle as solid and entrenched as were the laws of physics or of chemistry in this world of mine. For enchantment was a principle asserted time and time again in the olden fairy tales, in the ancient folklore, in a long line of fantasy writing that extended even into the present day. At one time people had believed in it, and for many, many years, and even in the present there were many of us who paid polite and not quite whimsical regard to this old belief, still reluctant to put aside the old beliefs and in many cases still half believing in them. How many people would go out of their way to avoid walking underneath a ladder? How many still felt a chill of apprehension when a black cat crossed their path? How many still carried a secret rabbit's foot, or if not a rabbit's foot, a certain lucky piece, a coin, perhaps, or some silly little emblem? How many people, in idle moments, still hunted four-leaf clovers? None of it was serious intent, perhaps, or only mock-seriously to cover up an unmodern attitude, but in their very acts betraying still the basic fear that lingered from the cave, the eternal human yen for protection against bad luck or black magic or the evil eye, or whatever other name one might put to it.

The Devil had complained that mankind's simple, thoughtless adages gave a lot of trouble to his world, which must accept them as laws and principles, and if such things as three times is a charm became actually operative in the Devil's world, then the simple matter of enchantment as a moving force became a certainty.

But while it was operative there, how could it be extended to this world of ours, where the principles of physics surely would hold an edge over the forces of enchantment? Although, come to think of it, this whole business of enchantment had its origins with man. Man had thought it up and passed it on to that other world and should the other world turn around and employ it against him, it would be no more than he deserved.

The whole thing didn't make any sort of sense when viewed within the logical context of the human world, but cars standing on the highways, the inoperative telephones, the silent radios and television sets did make a powerful kind of sense. Much as man might disbelieve in the efficiency of enchantment, there was here, all about me, evidence that it really worked.

And here was a situation, I told myself, that badly needed sense. If no cars would run, if no trains could operate, if all communications were cut off, then the country, in a few more days, would be heading for disaster. With transportation and communications gone, the economy of the nation would grind to a shuddering halt. Food would be in short supply in many urban centers, perhaps with an unreasoning rush of hoarding hastening that time. People would be hungry and the hungry hordes would stream out from the cities to seek food wherever they might find it.

Even now, I knew, twinges of panic must be in evidence. Facing the unknown, with the free flow of information halted, all manner of speculation and rumor would arise. In another day or two, spurred by those rumors, a full-fledged panic would be on.

The world of man, perhaps, had been struck a blow from which, if no answer could be found, it might not recover. The society, as it existed, was an intricate structure which rested, in large part, upon rapid transportation and instant communication. Pull those two foundation blocks out from under it and the whole frail house might come tumbling down. Within thirty days this proud structure would be gone and man would be hurled back into a state of barbarism, with roving bands seeking bases where they could sustain themselves.

I had one answer—an answer as to what had happened, but certainly no answer as to what to do about it. Thinking about it, I knew that even the answer I did have would be unacceptable. No one would believe it; no one, more than likely, would even give me the time to try to convince them it was true. The situation would give rise to a lot of crackpot explanations and mine would be only another one of them—another crackpot explanation.

The woman popped her head out of the kitchen. "I ain't seen you around," she said. "You must be a stranger."

I nodded.

"There are a lot of them in town," she said. "Came up off the highway. Some of them a right smart ways from home and no way to get back and . . ."

"The railroads must still be running."

She shook her head. "I don't think they are. Nearest one is twenty miles away and I heard someone say that they aren't running."

"Just where is this place?" I asked.

She eyed me suspiciously. "Seems to me," she said, "you don't know much of anything."

I didn't answer her and she finally told me what I'd asked. "Washington," she added, "is thirty miles down the road."

"Thanks," I said.

"It's a good, long walk," she said, "on a day like this. Going to be a scorcher before the day is over. You plan on walking all the way to Washington?"

"I'm considering it," I said.

She went back to her cooking.

Washington, thirty miles; Gettysburg, what would it be—sixty miles or more? And I had no assurance, I reminded myself, that Kathy would be in Gettysburg.

I thought about it—Washington or Gettysburg?

There were men in Washington who should know, who

had a right to know, what I could tell them, although it was most unlikely they would listen to me. There were men, some in fairly high positions, who were friends and others who were good acquaintances, but was there any one of them who would listen to the story that I had to tell? I checked a dozen of them mentally and there wasn't one of them who'd take me seriously. To begin with, they couldn't afford to; they couldn't subject themselves to the polite ridicule which would greet their lending any credence to what I had to say. In Washington, I was convinced, I could accomplish nothing more than butting my head against dozens of stone walls.

Knowing this, my very inclination shouted that I must get to Kathy's side as quickly as I could. If the world was going to go to pot, the two of us should be together when it smashed. She was the one person in the world who knew exactly what I knew; she was the only member of the human race who would understand the torment that I faced—the one person who would be sympathetic and willing to lend me help.

Although there was more than just sympathy and help; more than understanding. There was the remembrance of her body warm and sweet within my arms, the vision of her happy face looking up at me in the flaring light of the witch's fire. After many years, I thought, after many other women in strange and distant lands, here finally was Kathy. I had gone back to the land of boyhood, not certain it was right to go, not sure of what I'd find, and Kathy had been there.

The woman came in with the plate of eggs and bacon and I settled down to eating.

As I ate, an illogical idea crept into my mind and took hold of me. I tried to shake it off, for there was no basis for it and it was devoid of reason. But the more I tried to shake it off, the more it fastened to me—the conviction that I'd find Kathy, not in Gettysburg, but in Washington, in front of the fence that ran before the White House, feeding the White House squirrels.

We'd talked of the squirrels, I recalled, that night I'd walked her home and I tried to recall who had brought the

171

subject up and how we'd talked about it, but all that I could remember was that we'd talked about it and there had been nothing in that talk, I was fairly sure, that should have made me think what I was thinking now. But despite all that, I went on harboring that senseless, deep conviction, that I'd find Kathy at the White House. And now, to make it even worse, I held not only the deep conviction, but a sense of urgency. I had to get to Washington as quickly as I could for fear of missing her.

"Mister," said the woman behind the counter, "how did you get your face scratched up?"

"I fell," I told her.

"That was a nasty wallop you got alongside your head," she said. "Looks like there might be some infection in it. You ought to see a doctor."

"I haven't got the time," I said.

"Old Doc Bates is just down the street," she said. "He hasn't got much practice and you wouldn't have to wait. Old Doc, he ain't no great shakes, but he could fix that cut."

"I can't," I told her. "I have to get to Washington, as fast as I can go. I can't waste any time."

"I got some iodine out in the kitchen. I could wash it up and put on some iodine. There's probably a clean dish towel I could find that would keep the dirt out. You hadn't ought to run around with that cut infecting."

She watched me eat awhile and then she said, "It wouldn't be no trouble, mister. And I know how to do it. I was a nurse at one time. Must be something wrong with my head to have given it up to run a joint like this."

"You said your son had a bicycle," I said. "Would he consider selling it?"

"Well, now, I don't know," she said. "It's kind of rickety and it's not worth too much, but he sort of needs it to go and get the eggs."

"I'd pay a good price for it," I offered.

She hesitated; then she said, "I could ask him. But we can talk about it out there in the kitchen. I'll hunt up the iodine. I can't let you walk out of here with your head in that condition."

18

The woman had said it would be a scorcher and it was. Heat waves shimmered off the pavement and came wavering to meet me. The sky was a brassy bowl and there was no breath of breeze to stir the scorching air.

I'd had some trouble with the bike to start with, but within a couple of miles or so my body had recaptured some of the data programmed into it during boyhood days and I began to get the hang of it again. It wasn't easy, however; a lot better than walking, of course, and that would have been my choice.

I had told the woman that I'd pay a good price for the bike and she'd taken me at my word. A hundred dollars, which had taken almost all the money that I had. A hundred for an ancient contraption tied together with baling wire and stove bolts, worth, at the most, ten tucks. But it was either pay the price or walk, and I'd been in a hurry. And, I told myself, if the situation which now existed should continue, perhaps the bike was not really overpriced. If I could only have kept the horse, I'd have had a piece of property that would have been worthwhile. Horses and bikes might be the coming thing.

The highway was littered with stalled cars and trucks, with here and there a bus, but there weren't any people. Everyone who'd been on the stalled vehicles had had plenty of time to get off the road. It was a depressing sight, as if all those vehicles had been living things that had been killed and just left lying there; as if the highway itself, had been a living thing full of sound and movement and now was lying dead.

I kept pedaling along, wiping the sweat out of my eyes with my shirtsleeve and wishing that I had a drink of water, and after a time I saw that I was in the city's outskirts.

There were people, but no traffic was moving. Quite a lot of bicycles were on the street and I saw a few people who were using roller skates. There is nothing more ridiculous in the world than a man in a business suit, carrying an attaché case, and trying to be nonchalant as he proceeds down the street on a pair of roller skates. Everyone was either silently doing nothing—sitting on the curbs or on steps or out in their lawns and gardens—or going about their business in what seemed a rather desperate fashion.

I came to a little park, a typical Washington park, one block square with a statue in its center, benches set beneath the trees, an old lady feeding pigeons, and a drinking fountain. It was the drinking fountain that attracted me. The hours of pedaling in the sun had made my tongue feel like a mass of cotton that filled my entire mouth.

I didn't waste much time. I had a drink and rested for a moment on one of the benches, then got on the bike and set out again.

As I neared the White House I saw that a crowd had gathered, standing in a semicircle, filling the sidewalk and spilling out into the avenue, standing silently and staring, apparently at someone who stood beside the fence.

Kathy! I thought. For that was the exact place against the fence where I had expected her. But why should they be staring at her? What was going on?

I pedaled frantically up to the edge of the crowd and leaped off the bike. Letting it fall upon the sidewalk, I charged into the crowd, pushing and shoving. People swore at me and some pushed back and others shouted angrily, but I plowed my way through and finally staggered through the inner rank of people and out onto the sidewalk.

And there he stood—not Kathy, but the one, if I'd had good sense, I'd have expected to be there, Old Nick, His Satanic Majesty, the Devil.

He was dressed as I last had seen him, with his obscene belly hanging down over the dirty piece of cloth that afforded him a minimum of decency. He had his tail in his right hand and was using the barb of it as a toothpick to probe his mossy fangs. He leaned nonchalantly against the fence, with his cloven hoofs braced against a crack that ran along the concrete, and he was leering at the crowd in an infuriating manner. But at the sight of me, he dropped his tail forthwith and, advancing toward me, addressed me as a bosom pal for whom he had been waiting.

"Hail, the home-come hero!" he bugled, walking swiftly toward me with his arms outstretched. "Back from Gettysburg. I see that you got scotched. Where did you find the pretty baggage to tie up your head so becomingly?"

He went to throw his arms around me, but I jerked away. I was sore at him for being there when I'd expected to find Kathy.

"Where's Kathy?" I demanded. "I expected her."

"Oh, the little wench," he said. "You can rest your apprehensions. She is safe. At the great white castle on the hill. Above the witch's house. I expect you saw it."

"You lied to me," I told him, furiously. "You told me . . ."

"So I lied to you," he said, spreading his arms to indicate that it was of no consequence. "It is one of my most minor vices. What is a little lie among good friends? Kathy is safe so long as you play ball with me."

"Play ball with you!" I yelped, disgusted.

"You want the pretty cars to run," he said. "You want the radios to blat. You want the phones to ring."

The crowd was getting restless. It was pressing closer and while the people in it might not know what was going on, they were all ears when the Devil spoke about the cars and radios.

But the Devil ignored them. "A hero you can be," he said. "You can bring about negotiations. You can play the big shot."

I didn't want to be a hero. The crowd, I sensed, was getting ugly.

"We'll go in," the Devil said, "and talk turkey with

175

them." He made a thumb across his shoulder, pointing at the White House.

"We can't get in," I told him. "We can't just go walking in."

"Surely you have got a White House press card?"

"Yes, of course, I have. But that doesn't mean I can just walk in, anytime I wish. Especially with a bird like you in tow."

"You mean you can't get in?"

"Not the way you think."

"Look," he said, almost pleading with me, "you have to talk with them. You can shoot the proper lingo and you know the protocol. I can't do anything by myself. They would not listen to me."

I shook my head.

A couple of guards had left the gate and were walking down the sidewalk.

The Devil saw me looking at them.

"Trouble?" he demanded.

"I think it is," I said. "The guard probably has phoned the police—no, not phoned, I guess. But I imagine they have sent someone to tell the cops there might be trouble brewing."

He moved closer to me and spoke out of the corner of his mouth. "Trouble with cops I don't need," he said. He craned his neck to see the two guards. They still were walking toward us. He grabbed me by the arm. "Come on, let's go," he said.

The world went out from under me with a clap of thunder and in its place was darkness and the roar of heavy winds. Then we were in a large room with a long table running down the center of it and many men around the table. The man at the head of the table was the President.

Smoke was rising in tendrils from a scorched place in the carpet where I stood beside the Devil and the air was heavy with the smell of brimstone and of burning fabric. Someone was hammering fantically on the two doors that led into the room.

"Tell them, please," the Devil said, "that they can't get in. I'm afraid the doors are jammed."

A man with stars upon his shoulder leaped to his feet. His outraged bellow filled the room. "What is the meaning of this!"

"General," said the Devil, "please resume your seat and do your best to be at once an officer and a gentleman. No one will get hurt."

He flicked his tail ferociously to emphasize his words.

I looked quickly around the room to check my first impressions and I saw that they'd been right. Here we were, in the midst of a cabinet meeting—perhaps something more than a cabinet meeting, for there were others there, the director of the FBI, the head of the CIA, a sprinkling of high military brass, and a number of grim-faced men I did not recognize. Along a wall a group of very solemn and apparently learned men sat stiffly on a row of chairs.

Boy, I thought, we have done it now!

"Horton," said the Secretary of State, speaking gently to me, not flustered (he was never flustered), "what are you doing here? The last I knew of you, you were on a leave of absence."

"I took the leave," I said. "It seems it didn't last very long."

"You heard about Phil, of course."

"Yes, I heard of Phil."

The general was on his feet again and he, unlike the secretary, was a very flustered man. "If the Secretary of State will explain to me," he roared, "what is going on."

The pounding still was continuing, louder than ever now. As if the Secret Service boys were using chairs and tables to try to beat in the doors.

"This is most extraordinary," said the President, quietly, "but since these gentlemen are here, I would suspect they had some purpose in their coming. I suppose we should hear them out and then get on with business."

It was all ridiculous, of course, and I had the terrible feeling that I'd never left the Land of Imagination, that I still was in it, and that all this business of the President and his cabinet and the other people here was no more than a half-baked parody good for little more than a panel in a comic strip.

"I think," said the President to me, "that you must be Horton Smith, although I would not have recognized you."

"I was out fishing, Mr. President," I said. "I have had no time to change."

"Oh, that's quite all right," said the President. "We stand on no great ceremony here. But I don't know your friend."

"I'm not sure, sir, that he is my friend. He claims he is the Devil."

The President nodded sagely. "That is what I had thought, although it seemed farfetched. But if he is the Devil, what is he doing here?"

"I came," the Devil said, "to talk about a deal."

The Secretary of Commerce said, "About this difficulty with the cars . . ."

"But it's all insane!" protested the Secretary of Health, Education and Welfare. "I sit here and I see it happening and I tell myself it can't be happening. Even if there were such a personage as the Devil . . ." He turned to appeal to me. "Mr. Smith," he said, "you know this is not the way to go about it."

"Indeed I do," I said.

"I'll admit," said Commerce, "that these whole proceedings are most irregular, but this is an unusual situation. If Mr. Smith and his sulfurous friend have any information, we should listen to them. We've listened to great numbers of other people, including our scientific friends," and he made a sweeping gesture to indicate the men ranged in the chairs along the wall, "and we haven't heard a thing except a large array of people telling us that what has happened is impossible. The scientific community informs us that these happenings defy all laws of physics and that they are frankly fuddled. And the engineers have told us . . ."

"But the Devil!" bellowed the man with the stars upon his shoulders.

"If he is the Devil," said the Secretary of Interior.

"My friends," the President said, wearily, "there was another president—a great wartime president—who, upon

178

being chided for doing business with an unsavory foreign character, said that to span a stream he'd walked across a bridge with the Devil. And here is another president who will not shy from dealing with the Devil if it shows the way out of our dilemma."

The President looked across the room at me. "Mr. Smith," he asked, "can you explain to us just what in hell is going on?"

"Mr. President," protested HEW, "this is too ridiculous to waste our time upon. If the press should ever get a whiff of what went on within this room . . ."

The Secretary of State snorted. "Little good it would do them if they did. How would they get it out? I presume that all press wires are down. And, in any case, Mr. Smith is of the press, and if he so wishes, no matter what we do we can't keep it quiet."

"It's a waste of time," said the general.

"We've had an entire morning of wasted time," Commerce pointed out.

"I'd waste more of it," I told them. "I can tell you what it's all about, but you won't believe a word of it."

"Mr. Smith," said the President, "I would hate to have to beg you."

I snapped at him. "Sir, you do not have to beg me."

"Then will you and that friend of yours pull chairs up to the table and tell us what you came to say."

I walked across the room to get one of the chairs he had indicated and the Devil clumped along beside me, switching his tail excitedly. The hammering on the doors had stopped.

As I walked I could feel holes being bored into my back by the eyes of the men around the table. For the love of God, I thought, what a spot to be in—sitting in a room with the President and his cabinet, brass from the Pentagon, a panel of outstanding scientists, and various advisers. And the worst thing about it was that before I was through with them they'd tear me to tiny ribbons. I had wondered just how I could go about finding anyone in authority, or close to authority, who would sit still long enough to listen to me. And now I had those people who were about to listen to me—not a single person, but a whole room full of them—and I was scared to death. Health, Education and Welfare had been shooting off his mouth, and so had the general, while most of the others had sat stolidly in place, but I had no doubt before it was all over, some of the others would join in.

I pulled the chair over to the table and the President said to me, "Just go ahead and tell us what you know. From having watched you at times on television, I know you can give us a lucid and no doubt interesting account."

I wondered how to start, how to tell them, in a minimum of time, the story of what had happened in the last few days. Then, suddenly, I knew the only way to do it—pretend that I was in front of a microphone and camera and that I was doing nothing more than I had done for years. Except it wouldn't be all that easy. In a studio I would have had time to outline in my mind exactly what to say, would have had a script to help out in the rough spots. Here I was on my own and I didn't like it much, but I was stuck with it and there was nothing I could do but go through with it the best way that I could.

They all were looking at me and a good many of them, I knew, were angry with me for being about to insult their intelligence, and there were others who plainly were amused, knowing very well there was no such thing as a Devil and waiting for the punch line. And I think, as well, that some of them were frightened, but that made little difference, for they had been frightened before the Devil and myself had come into the room.

"There are some things I am going to tell you," I said, "that you can check on." I looked at the Secretary of State. "Phil's death, for instance." I saw his start of surprise, but I didn't give him a chance to say anything, but kept right on. "For the most part, however," I told them, "there is no way of checking. I'll tell you the truth, or as close to the truth as I can come. As for believing any of it, or all of it, that is up to you . . ."

Now that I had made a start, it was easy to go on. I pretended that I wasn't in the cabinet room, but that I was in a studio and that when I got through with what I had to say, I'd get up and leave.

They sat and listened quietly, although there were several times that some of them stirred uneasily, as if they were ready to break in on me. But the President raised his hand and shushed them and allowed me to go on. I didn't check my time, but I would guess it didn't take much more than fifteen minutes. I packed a lot of meat into what I had to say; I left out everything except the basics of it.

When I was finished, no one said anything for a moment and I sat there, looking around the table at them.

Finally, the FBI director stirred. "Most interesting," he said.

"Yes, isn't it," said the general, acidly.

"What I gather," said Commerce, "is that this friend of yours objects to the fact that we have introduced so many diverse elements into this mythical land of his that we've played hob with any attempt to set up a decent kind of government."

"Not a government," I said quickly, aghast that the man should think in terms of a government for such a place as I had described. "A culture. Perhaps, you'd call it a way of life. A purpose—for there seems no purpose in the land. Each goes his merry, zany way. There is no direction. You'll understand, of course, that I had only a few hours there and so I can't . . ."

Treasury turned a look of horror upon Commerce. "You can't mean," he cried, "that you place any credence in this—this fairy tale—this . . ."

"I don't know if I do or not," said Commerce. "We have here a credible witness who, I am convinced, would not give perjured testimony."

"He's been duped!" cried Treasury.

"Or it's a publicity stunt of some sort," declared HEW.

"If you gentlemen will permit me," said State, "there is one statement that struck me rather forceably. Philip Freeman died, so the coroner said, of a heart attack. There was some very puzzling talk that he'd been shot by an arrow—an arrow fired by a man dressed as an ancient

181

archer might have been. But no one, of course, believed it. It was too incredible. Just as this story we have heard seems incredible and if so . . ."

"You believe this story?" HEW demanded.

"It's hard to believe," said State, "but I would warn against sweeping it all aside, brushing it underneath the carpet without a second glance. We should, at least, discuss it."

The general said, "Perhaps we should ask our panel of distinguished scientists what they think of it." He swung around in his chair and nodded at the line of men in chairs against the wall.

Slowly one of them got to his feet. He was a fussy and feeble old man, white-haired and, in a strange manner, very dignified. He spoke carefully, making little motions with his blue-veined hands. "I may not speak for all my colleagues," he said, "and if I do not, I presume they will correct me. But in my view, my most considered view, I must say that a situation such as has been outlined here violates all known scientific tenets. I'd say it was impossible."

He sat down as carefully as he had gotten up, putting down his hands to grasp the chair arms firmly before he lowered himself into the seat.

Silence filled the room. One or two of the scientists nodded their heads, but none of the others stirred.

The Devil said to me, "These stupid jerks don't believe a word of it!"

The room was quiet and he said it loud enough so that all could hear him and while there was ample reason to believe that at one time or another, politics being what they are, they'd all been characterized as stupid jerks by someone, this was the first time, more than likely, they'd been called it to their faces.

I shook my head at him, both as a rebuke for the language he had used and to let him know that no, they did not believe it. I knew they didn't dare believe it; anyone who believed it would be laughed out of public office.

The Devil leaped to his feet and banged a massive, hairy fist upon the table. Little jets of smoke spurted from his ears.

"You created us," he yelled at them. "With your dirty little evil minds and your beautifully fuzzy minds and your fumbling, uncertain, yearning, fearful minds you created us and the world you put us in. You did it without knowing it and for that you can't be blamed, although one would think that personages so clever with the physics and the chemistry would have run to earth these impossible things your savants say can't happen. But now that you do know, now that the knowing has been forced upon you, you are morally obligated to come up with a remedy to the deplorable conditions you have forced upon us. You can . . ."

The President sprang to his feet and, like the Devil, thumped the table with his fist—although the total effect was lost since no smoke spouted from his ears.

"Monsieur Devil," he shouted, "I want some answers from you. You say you stopped the cars and the radios and . . ."

"You're damned right I stopped them," roared the Devil. "All over the world I stopped them, but it was a warning only, a showing of what could be done. And I was humane about it. The cars came to smooth and even stops and not a soul was injured. The planes I let get to the ground before I made them not to run. The factories I left working so there would be jobs and wages and goods still being made . . ."

"But without transportation we are dead," yelled Agriculture, who had been silent heretofore. "If food can't be moved, the people will starve. If goods can't move, business will come to a standstill."

"Our armies in the field," the general cried. "They have no planes nor armor and communications are cut off . . ."

"You ain't seen nothing yet," the Devil told them. "Next time around the wheel will be outlawed. No wheel will turn. No factories, no bicycles, no roller skates, no . . ."

"Monsieur Devil, please," screamed the President, "will you lower your voice? Will all of us lower our voices? There is nothing gained in screaming. We must be reasonable. I had one question and now I have another. You say you did this. Now tell us how you did it."

"Why, I," the Devil stammered, "why, I just did it, that is all. I said let it happen and it happened. I do a lot of things that way. You see, you wrote it into me and you thought it into me and you talked it into me. A devil can do anything at all, so long as it is bad. I doubt exceedingly I'd be so successful doing good."

"Enchantment, gentlemen," I told them. "That is the only answer for it. And don't blame the Devil for it; we thought it up ourselves."

The old gentleman who had spoken for the scientists lurched to his feet. He raised clenched fists above his head. "Enchantment," he squeaked. "There can't be enchantment. There is no law of science . . ." He meant to say more, but his voice choked and he stood for a moment, fighting for breath and voice, but giving up, sat down.

"Maybe not," the Devil said. "Maybe not any science law. But what care we for science? The wheel next, then electricity and after that, most likely, fire, although I haven't thought that far ahead. And once that is done, back to the feudal manor, back to the good old Dark Ages, where there was some honest thinking done and . . ."

"Now, sir," said the President, "another question, please, if you have done with threats."

"Most excellent sir," said the Devil, trying very hard to be polite, "I do not deal in threats. I only tell what can be done and what shall be done and . . ."

"But why?" asked the President. "What exactly is your grievance?"

"Grievance!" bellowed the Devil, in a rage and forgetful of politeness. "You ask me for grievance. Horton Smith, who has a wound from Gettysburg. who jousted bare-handed with Quixote, who chased a vicious witch through

184

a fearsome woods, has outlined my grievance."

As a sign of his honest reason, he let his voice sink from a bellow to a roar. "Once," he said, "our land was peopled by a hardy folk, some of them honestly good and some of them as honestly evil. I kid you not, my friends; I was and am one of the evil ones. But at least we had purpose and between the good and bad, between the imps and fairies, we made a life of it. But now what have we got? I'll tell you what we have. We have Li'l Abner and Charley Brown and Pogo. We have Little Orphan Annie and Dagwood Bumstead and the Bobbsey Twins, Horatio Alger, Mr. Magoo, Tinkerbell, Mickey Mouse, Howdy Doody . . ."

The President waved him silent. "I think you have made your point," he said.

"They have no character," said the Devil. "They have no flavor nor any style. They are vapid things. There's not an honestly evil one among them and none is really good—the goodness that is in them is enough to turn one's stomach. I ask you in great sincerity how one is to build a worthwhile civilization with inhabitants such as that?"

"This gentleman's stomach," said HEW, "is not the only one's that's turned. I am aghast that we sit here and listen to this buffoonery."

"Just a little more," said the President. "I'm trying to make something out of this. With your indulgence, please."

"I suppose," the Devil said, "that you are wondering now what can be done about it."

"Precisely," said the President.

"You can put an end to all this foolishness. You can halt the Li'l Abners and the Mickey Mouses and the Howdy Doodies. You can return to honest fantasy. You can think about some evil things and others that are good and you can believe in them . . ."

Agriculture was on his feet. "I have never in my life," he yelled, "heard such an infamous suggestion. He is suggesting thought control. He would have us dictate entertainment values and he would have us throttle artistic and

185

literary creativity. And even if we agreed to do this, how would we go about it? Laws and edicts would not be enough. A secret campaign would have to be launched, a most secret one, and I would guess it would be impossible to keep it secret for longer than three days. But even if we could, it would take billions of dollars and years of Madison Avenue's most devious and devoted effort and I don't think even then that it would catch on. These are not the Dark Ages, the honest thought of which this gentleman seems to admire so greatly. We cannot bring our people, or the people of the world, to believe again in devils or in imps, or in angels, either. I propose that we close out this discussion."

"My friend," said Treasury, "takes this incident too seriously. I cannot bring myself, nor, I suspect, can many others in this room, to regard it as of any validity at all. To give the color of acceptance to this ridiculous situation by debating it on even the most hypothetical grounds seems to me to be degrading and not in keeping with the dignity of orderly procedure."

"Hear! Hear!" the Devil said.

"We have taken enough of your impudence," the FBI said to the Devil. "It is not in the best American tradition for a council of state to be insulted by such outbursts of malicious nonsense delivered by something, or someone, who can have no actual basis in fact."

"That does it!" the Devil raged. "No basis in fact, you say. I'll show you nincompoops. Next comes the wheel and electricity and then I will be back and we have a better basis, maybe, for some forthright dealing."

Saying which, he reached out and grabbed me by the arm. "Leave us go," he said.

We went, no doubt in a flash of evil-smelling light and smoke. In any case, the world went away again and there was the blackness and the howling of the winds and when the blackness fell away we were back on the sidewalk outside the White House fence.

"Well," the Devil said, triumphantly, "I guess I told them, kid. I took the pompous hides off their four-flushing backs. Did you see their faces when I called them nin-compoops?"

"Yes, you did well," I said, disgusted. "You have all the finesse of a hog."

He rubbed his hands together. "And now," he said, "the wheels."

"Lay off it," I warned him. "You'll wreck this world of ours and then what will happen to that precious world of yours . . ."

But the Devil wasn't listening to me. He was looking over my shoulder and down the street and there was a funny look upon his face. The crowd that had ringed the Devil in when I first had found him had disappeared, but there were a number of people in the park across the street and these people now were shouting in an excited fashion.

I swung around to look.

Less than half a block away and bearing down upon us with great rapidity was Don Quixote astride the running bag of bones that served him as a charger. His helm was down and the shield was up. The leveled lance was aglitter in the sun. Behind him Sancho Panza applied an enthusiastic whip to his donkey, which humped along in a stiff-legged gait not unlike a startled rabbit. While he applied the whip with one hand, Sancho Panza held the other arm out stiffly to one side, clutching a bucket. There was some sort of liquid in the bucket and it slopped alarmingly as the donkey tried its best to keep up with the storming charger. And behind the two of them came a prancing unicorn, shining white in the brilliant sunlight, with its slender horn a breathtaking lance of silver. It moved daintily and easily and was a thing of utter grace, and seated upon it, riding it sidesaddle fashion, was Kathy Adams.

The Devil reached out a hand for me, but I knocked his arm away and made a grab at him. I clutched him about the middle and as I did so I kicked my foot backward, forcing it between two iron palings of the fence. I didn't really think what I was doing; I didn't plan it, and I'm not sure I knew at the time exactly why I did it. But apparently there was some subconscious thought inside of

187

me that informed me that it just possibly might work. If I could divert the Devil from taking off to some other place for no longer than a second, Don Quixote would be down upon him and, if his aim were true, he'd have the Devil spitted on his lance. And there was also something about being securely anchored if I were to do it and another something about the effect of iron upon the Devil, and that, I suppose, was the reason I stuck my foot between the palings.

The Devil was squirming to get away, but I hung onto him, with my arms locked about his middle. His hide stank and my face, where I had it pressed against his chest, was wet with his greasy sweat. He was struggling and cursing horribly and beating at me with his fists, but out of the corner of one eye I saw the lance point flashing in toward us. The beat of clopping hooves came closer and then the lance point struck with a squashy sound and the Devil fell away. I let go of him and fell upon the sidewalk, with my foot still between the palings.

I twisted around and saw that the lance had caught the Devil in the shoulder and had him pinned against the fence. He was squirming and mewling. He waved his arms and froth ran out of the corners of his mouth.

Don Quixote raised a hand and tried to flip his visor up. It stuck. He wrenched at it so hard that he jerked the entire helmet off his head. It flew from his fingers and clanked upon the sidewalk.

"Varlet," Don Quixote cried, "I call on you to yield and to give your bounden pledge you will henceforth desist from any further interference in the world of man."

"To hell and damnation with you," the Devil raged. "I will yield to no busybody of a do-gooder that spends his time sniffing out crusades. And of all of them, there is none worse than you, Quixote. You can sense a good deed a million light years off and you are off hell-bent to do it. And I'll have none of it. You understand that, I'll have none of it!"

Sancho Panza had leaped off the donkey and was running forward with the bucket which, I now saw, had a dipper in it. In front of the Devil, he halted and with the dipper splashed some of the liquid on the Devil. The liquid boiled and hissed and the Devil writhed in agony.

"Water!" Sancho Panza cried in glee. "Blessed by the good St. Patrick and most potent stuff."

He let the Devil have another dipper of it. The Devil writhed and screamed.

"Pledge!" Don Quixote shouted.

"I yield," the Devil yelled. "I yield and pledge."

"And further pledge," said Don Quixote grimly, "that all mischief you here have caused will end—and that immediately."

"I will not," the Devil screamed. "Not all my work undone!"

Sancho Panza flung the dipper on the sidewalk and clutched the pail in both his hands, poised to hurl its entire contents on the Devil.

"Hold!" the Devil shouted. "Avast that cursed water! I do entirely yield and pledge everything you ask."

"Then," Don Quixote said, with a certain courtliness, "our mission here is done."

I didn't see them go. There wasn't even a flicker of their going. They just suddenly were gone. There was no Devil, no Don Quixote, no Sancho Panza and no unicorn. But Kathy was running toward me and I thought it strange she could run so well with her ankle sprained. I tried to jerk my foot free of the fence so I could get up to greet her, but the foot was tightly stuck between the palings and I could not get it loose.

She went down on her knees beside me. "We're home again!" she cried. "Horton, we are home!"

She leaned down to kiss me and across the street the crowd cheered loudly and ribaldly at the kiss.

"My foot is stuck," I said.

"Well, pull it loose," she told me, smiling through tears of happiness.

I tried to pull it loose and couldn't. It hurt when I pulled on it. She got up and went to the fence and tried to work it free, but it still stayed stuck.

"I think the ankle's swelling," she said and sat down upon the sidewalk, laughing. "The two of us," she cried.

"We have something with our ankles. First mine, now yours."

"Your ankle is all right," I said.

"They had magic at the castle," she told me. "A most wonderful old magician with a long white beard and a funny cap and gown with stars all over them. It was the nicest place I've ever seen. So genteel and polite. I could have stayed forever if you had been there with me. And the unicorn. He was the nicest, sweetest thing. You saw the unicorn?"

"I saw the unicorn," I said.

"Horton, who are those men coming down across the lawn?"

I had been so busy looking at her and so glad that she was back, that I'd not been looking at the lawn. When I did look, I saw them. The President was in the lead, running toward the fence, and behind him streamed the other people who'd been in the room.

The President reached the fence and stopped. He regarded me with something less than friendliness.

"Horton," he demanded, "what the hell is going on out here?"

"My foot is caught," I said.

"To hell with your foot," he said. "That isn't what I mean. I swear I saw a knight and a unicorn."

The others were crowding close up against the fence.

A guard shouted from up by the gate. "Hey! Everybody look! There's a car coming down the street!"

Sure enough, there was.

"But what about his foot?" Kathy asked, indignantly. "We can't get it loose and his ankle's swelling. I'm afraid it's sprained."

"Someone had better get a doctor," said the Secretary of State. "If the cars are running, the phones may be working, too. How are you feeling, Horton?"

"I'm all right," I said.

"And get someone down here with a hacksaw," said the President. "For the love of God, we got to saw his foot loose."

So I stayed there on the sidewalk and Kathy sat beside

190

me, waiting for the doctor and the hacksaw man.

Disregarding the crowd inside the fence, some of the White House squirrels came sneaking out on the sidewalk to see what was going on. They sat up most daintily, with their forepaws crossed upon their chest, begging for a handout.

And the cars, more and more of them, went on rolling past.

AND DON'T MISS THESE

SCIENCE FICTION NOVELS FROM BERKLEY!

THE POWER OF X
  by ARTHUR SELLINGS   (X1801—60¢)

RETIEF AND THE WARLORDS
  by KEITH LAUMER   (X1800—60¢)

THE WORLD OF NULL-A
  by A. E. VAN VOGT   (S1802—75¢)

GLORY ROAD
  by ROBERT A. HEINLEIN   (N1809—95¢)

FIVE TO TWELVE
  by EDMUND COOPER   (X1768—60¢)

DR. ORPHEUS
  by IAN WALLACE   (S1767—75¢)

Send for a free list of all our books in print

These books are available at your local newsstand, or send
price indicated plus 10¢ per copy to cover mailing costs to
Berkley Publishing Corporation, 200 Madison Avenue,
New York, N.Y. 10016

S0-BNS-366

ONE WARM FOX

NICK BUTTERWORTH

Collins

An Imprint of HarperCollins*Publishers*

"Shoo! Go on, shoo!" said Percy the park keeper. "This isn't bird seed. Shoo!"

Percy was sowing some wild flower seed on a patch of bare earth. But a bunch of rooks who had suddenly appeared were trying to gobble up the seed as fast as Percy could scatter it.

"And you're not much help," said
Percy to a rather saggy-looking
scarecrow he had made. He sighed
and tried to cover the last of the seed
with his rake.

When Percy got back to his hut,
he found his friend the fox sitting
on the steps. Next to the fox there was
a parcel.

"Hello," said Percy. "I see
the postman has been."

P ercy picked up the parcel and
looked at the writing.
"Oh dear," he said.

" W hat's the matter?" said the fox.
"Don't you like parcels?"
"Not from Auntie Joyce," said Percy.
"She knits things. This will be another
pullover or a scarf or something. I've
got a collection."

Percy began to open the parcel.
"She's very kind," said Percy, "but
somehow, the things she knits. . .well,
they don't really suit me. Not my sort
of colours. Either that or they don't fit."

"**P**erhaps they'd fit me," said the fox.
"I was a bit chilly last night."
Percy unwrapped the rest of the parcel.

"Well, this will keep your ears warm,"
he chuckled, and he tossed the fox a
woolly balaclava. "Very nice, but a bit
small for me, I think."

The fox pulled on the balaclava.
He looked a bit disappointed.
"I was thinking more of a pullover,"
he said. "This is squashing my ears."

P ercy smiled.
   "Follow me," he said.
"Pardon?" said the fox.

"I said follow me," Percy repeated
loudly, and he led the fox into his hut.

Percy brought out an old suitcase from under his bed. He blew the dust off it and opened it.

"How about this?" Percy held up one of Auntie Joyce's pullovers. The fox put it on.

"It fits!" said the fox happily.

"So it does," said Percy with a chuckle.
"In that case, help yourself. I'm
just going to check my wild flower patch."

Percy wasn't gone for long. As he walked back towards his hut, he didn't look too pleased.

But, as soon as Percy opened the door, his face changed.

"Everything fits!" said the fox.
Percy roared with laughter.

"You can't go about like that!" he said.
"Anyway, you'll be much too hot. You'll
cook!"

"It is a bit warm," admitted the fox.
"I just thought, at night, you know. . ."

"You can keep the pullover," said
Percy, "but I think you should take off
the rest. Besides, I think I know someone
that these things might suit."

The next morning, Percy was out working in the park when he met the fox again.

"How were you last night?" asked Percy.

"As warm as toast!" said the fox. "How is your wild flower patch? Are those rooks still being a nuisance?"

"I can't understand it," Percy chuckled.
"They haven't been near the place!"

NICK BUTTERWORTH

Nick Butterworth was born in North London in 1946 and grew up in a sweet shop in Essex. He now lives in Suffolk with his wife Annette and their two children, Ben and Amanda.

The inspiration for the Percy the Park Keeper books came from Nick Butterworth's many walks through the local park with the family dog, Jake. The stories have now been made into a stunning animated television series, available on video from HIT Entertainment plc.

Look out for all Percy's adventures:

ONE SNOWY NIGHT · AFTER THE STORM
THE RESCUE PARTY · THE SECRET PATH
THE TREASURE HUNT

THE CROSS RABBIT · THE FOX'S HICCUPS
THE BADGER'S BATH · THE HEDGEHOG'S BALLOON
ONE WARM FOX · THE OWL'S LESSON